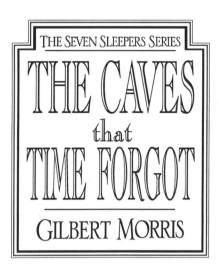

THE SEVEN SLEEPERS SERIES

THE CAVES
that
TIME FORGOT

GILBERT MORRIS

MOODY PRESS

CHICAGO

© 1995 by
GILBERT L. MORRIS

ISBN: 0-8024-3684-6

1 3 5 7 9 10 8 6 4 2

Printed in the United States of America

To Andy Blackwell
A very special young man

Contents

1
Another Quest

I'd give anything if I could go to a beauty shop."

Abbie Roberts was a petite girl of thirteen. She had blonde hair, and her blue eyes gave off sparks as she ran her hands through her long locks. "And a manicure," she added. "Look at these fingernails! They'll never be the same again!"

Sarah Collingwood, sitting across from Abbie, was one year older. She did not have Abbie's spectacular good looks, but she was small and graceful with large brown eyes and black hair.

"Abbie," she said with some irritation, "you might as well forget about such things as beauty shops. You may have had things like that in Oldworld, but they're gone forever."

The two girls sat at the mouth of a small cave and had been staring out into the late afternoon dusk. Both wore clothes that were much the worse for wear. Abbie's blue dress had a torn skirt and was practically stiff with dirt. Sarah's garb was not much better—a pair of jeans with ragged cuffs and a tan shirt with most of the buttons replaced by pins. Both were hot and tired and hungry.

Abbie glared. "I think this camping out is terrible. I liked it much better when we were at Camelot—or even down in Atlantis." She picked up a cloth, went and dipped it into the small stream that ran beside the cave, then wrung out the excess water. Wiping her face, she protested again. "I need some face cream. My skin's getting as rough as rhinoceros hide."

"We'll just have to make the best of it." Sarah looked again into the gathering darkness. "I wish the boys would come back. It's going to be dark soon, and I'll bet there are wild animals around here."

Abigail said abruptly, "Let's wash our hair. I can't stand it when my hair gets stiff with dirt like this."

"We don't have any soap." Sarah gave her companion a critical look. "I wish you'd just learn to be patient, Abbie. We knew this was going to be a hard trip."

The Seven Sleepers had just completed an adventure at a strange place called Camelot. Their heads were still filled with visions of ladies and jousting knights and even dragons.

It was the sort of adventure they would have enjoyed in their earlier lives. But their time in Oldworld had been cut short by a terrible war. They had survived only because their parents placed them in sleep capsules. Years passed, and the world changed completely so that when they came forth they were shocked to find themselves living in the midst of strange creatures and alien landscapes. Then they were called to spread the news that Goél, a strange shadowy figure, was going to bring order and peace to Nuworld, as it was called.

"When do you think we'll get out of this terrible forest?" Abbie asked irritably.

"I don't know."

"Well, I think Goél could have arranged things a little better. If we have to go from place to place, I don't see why he can't give us better transportation."

Sarah rose to her feet suddenly, biting her lip. She was tired and hungry, and Abigail's constant complaining got on her nerves. She walked downstream a few feet, stopped and listened, then said, "Someone's coming!"

Abbie scrambled up and came to stand beside Sarah. Her eyes grew large, and she whispered, "I hope it's

8

them—but it could be anybody out in the middle of this forest."

The two girls peered into the wall of huge trees that flanked the stream.

The voices Sarah had heard grew louder, and then, as three young men stepped out from the shadows, she cried with relief, "It's Josh—and the others! I hope they brought something to eat." She ran across the small clearing to the leader. "Josh, are you all right? We were getting worried."

Josh Adams was fourteen. He was tall and gangling, but there was a promise of strength and grace in his growing form. He was not handsome, and yet there was reliability and steadiness in his face. He had auburn hair that caught the last rays of the sun, and blue eyes. He had been the first Sleeper, the one called to find the rest. He had grown especially close to Sarah.

"Sure, we're OK, Sarah. Just tired and ready to eat."

One of the other boys held out a sack. "We've got three rabbits," he said. "That'll be enough to eat tonight."

"Oh, good, Jake," Sarah said. "Give them to me. I'll clean them."

Jake Garfield was thirteen, a Jewish boy, small with red hair and intense brown eyes. He handed over the bag. "I wish they'd been yearling calves though. I'm hungry enough to eat one."

The other boy was the smallest of the three. He was twelve, and his black face was split now by a gleaming white smile. "I'll clean those rabbits, Sarah," he said. "I don't mind."

"Oh, thank you, Wash. But you all go rest while Abbie and I do the cooking."

The boys threw themselves down in front of the cave, groaning with relief.

9

Sarah borrowed a knife from Josh and dressed the rabbits, gutting them while Abbie quickly gave herself to building a fire. She managed to cut some saplings into sticks, and the girls soon had the game roasting over the yellow flame.

When the rabbits were almost done, two more boys came in. Dave, the tallest of the Sleepers and the oldest at fifteen, called out, "We've got another rabbit if we need it." He was athletic, very handsome. He had yellow hair and blue eyes and walked with a springy step.

"Reb," he said to his companion, "that was a good shot. I don't think I could have gotten that one."

The final Sleeper was the most spectacular of all. At fourteen, he was very tall. He had light blue eyes and pale, bleached hair. He wore a Stetson as only a cowboy would wear it. In fact, he had been a kind of cowboy, growing up in Texas in his old life. He grinned now and said, "Shucks, that wasn't no shot at all, Dave. If I'd of had my 30-30, I'd of got that deer we seen a ways back."

"Well, I wish you had it." Dave sat down beside the three boys at the cave mouth. "I wish Goél would let us have rifles. Sure would make life simpler."

All seven young people showed the marks of long travel. They had had time for only quick splashes of water on their faces as far as bathing was concerned, and now they were about to find themselves back in a civilization again.

For a while, Dave did most of the talking. He spoke about their recent adventures, and he grinned at Reb. "Do we still have to call you 'Sir Reb' now that we're out of Camelot?"

"Oh, I reckon not."

Reb had been the hero of their adventure there. A natural horseman and having been a rider all his life, he had been able to do things in that country that the others could not.

Now the darkness closed about them, and the flickering firelight reflected on Reb's pale blue eyes. "I liked that place," he said slowly, "about as well as any place I ever seen."

"Even better than Texas?" Jake asked.

"Well, maybe not that good—but except for Texas I guess it was about the best place I was ever at."

"I think you just had a case of puppy love." Josh grinned across the fire. "I can't blame you though. That princess sure was a pretty thing, and she sure was gone on you."

Reb's face reddened, but he said nothing. Finally he looked up. "You reckon we'll ever get back there?"

Sarah tested one of the roasting rabbits with Josh's knife. "I hope so. I hope *you* do anyhow. It seemed like you were born for a place like that—horses and jousting. A little bit like the days of the old West." Again she poked at the rabbit. "I think this is about done. Come and get it."

They gathered around, and Sarah and Abbie cut up the rabbits and served them. Then they all sat back, handling the hot meat gingerly, listening to the silence of the forest as they ate.

"Well, that was good," Wash said, licking his fingers. "Still wish that rabbit had been as big as the deer that got away. My stomach thinks my throat's been cut." He looked over at Josh. "How much longer you think it'll be before we get out of this woods?"

"I don't know." Josh pulled the last fragment of meat off a bone, then tossed the bone out into the grass. "Maybe a day or two. And then what?"

His question produced a moody atmosphere, and each Sleeper seemed to be thinking of all that had gone past.

"I'd like to have a little R & R," Reb said.

11

Jake looked up. "What's that?"

"Rest and recreation." Reb grinned tiredly. "It looks like we could use a little vacation, but I don't know if we'll get it."

Sarah opened her mouth to comment. But before she could speak, a familiar voice broke the silence.

"I realize you're all tired, and I wish that you could have more rest."

The suddenness and unexpectedness of the voice shocked her. Then a tall figure stepped out of the darkness into the firelight, and Josh cried out, "Goél!"

"Goél!" the rest echoed, and all jumped to their feet to greet their guest.

The man was dressed in a gray robe that reached to his knees. His feet were clad with heavy sandals, and the cowl for covering his head was thrown back. He carried a staff in his hand, and there was strength and patience in his face as well as great gentleness.

He let the Sleepers have their way for a moment, smiling at their greetings, then said, "Sit down, my friends. Rest."

He himself remained standing. His craggy face caught the light of the fire, and a smile still touched his lips. "You did well on your quest to Camelot. All of you."

Reb ducked his head. "Well, I made a mess of part of it," he mumbled. "I let myself get taken in by that there sorceress."

Goél's expression did not change. "But you have learned, my son, something about how to defend yourself against the powers of darkness. It is a lesson that you can put to good use on your next quest."

"Are we really going on another journey?" Josh burst out.

"Do you feel strong enough for it?" Goél asked.

Dave said at once, "We're tired, but if you give the word, we'll go. Anywhere you say, Goél."

The strange man smiled yet again. "That is good, my son, and for your bold speech you shall be the leader on the next adventure."

Sarah thought the others looked surprised, especially Josh. From the beginning he had been the leader of the Sleepers. He blinked his eyes in shock. He said nothing, but she could read the disappointment in his face.

Then Goél was speaking, and all paid careful heed. "You have been obedient to my commands. You have learned much. But the next task I will put to you will demand every bit of strength you have, for the people to whom I send you now are quite different."

"As different as the people of Atlantis that live under the sea?" Wash asked. "They were pretty strange folks, I thought."

"And the people at Camelot?" Abigail said. "They were unusual too. How can anybody be more different?"

For a time silence fell over the small, open space where the little fire gleamed. Far off a bird cried, and the trees about them seemed to breathe.

Goél's voice was low, and Sarah listened carefully, knowing it was likely they were going to face danger.

"The Dark Power," Goél said slowly, "is strong and is growing stronger. Those who are my servants, such as yourself, are small in number. They must make up in courage what they lack in numbers. All over Nuworld the Dark Lord is desperately striving to stamp out all of the things that I value—courage, goodness, and love most of all. I am about to send you to a people who know little about such things."

"What kind of people are they?" Josh piped up.

"Not like you," Goél said. "At least you will think they are not. They will have different values, and you will

13

have to convince them that the things you believe in are important. You must teach them that if they are to survive, they must stand against the evil that darkens the world. They need," he said firmly, "to learn about dignity and honor and love. They must learn to treat others as they themselves would want to be treated."

He spoke for a long time. Sarah sat listening, trying to store up his words.

Finally Goél said, "These people are simple. I do not wish that you would dazzle them with your superior knowledge or with inventions that might bring destruction to them. When you go to them, you must become in some ways as simple as they are. Only by humility will you win them. I can give you encouragement and hope, but the path that you must tread will not be easy."

Goél drew the cowl up over his head so that his face was shrouded. He reached into a pocket of his cloak and drew forth a paper and a leather bag. "Here is money for your journey and a map. Follow it. You will discover this people when you reach this point—here." He pointed. "Good-bye for now, but I will not be far away from you."

Then he turned and walked off into the darkness. The Sleepers looked after him until the gloom swallowed him up.

"Well," Wash said, "I guess that answers any questions about our getting a vacation." He sat down, looked at the carcass of one of the rabbits, almost picked clean, and shook his head. "I sure wish you was as big as a deer," he said sadly. "I could eat you all myself."

2

Voyage to Nowhere

W ell, there it is!" Dave exclaimed, looking out across the vast expanse of gray ocean. "I thought we'd never get here!"

The Sleepers had forged their way through dense woods and along narrow, twisting roads for more than a week. They camped beside the road each night and had been fortunate enough to find food at a few small villages.

"I just hope there's a shop where I can buy something," Abbie said with irritation. She brushed at her clothes ineffectively. "I wouldn't wear these old rags to a rummage sale!"

"That looks like a village over there." Josh nodded in the direction of the shoreline. "From the looks of all those ships, it's some kind of port. So I'm sure we can find something. Come on!"

Dave sent Josh a quick look and said sharply, "I think we'd better get organized before we go into the village."

Sarah as well as several other Sleepers had noticed that Dave was jealous of his new authority.

Wash grinned at Reb. "Give a man a top job, and he'll pretty soon show you what he is, won't he?"

But Abbie was so anxious to get to a store that she put a hand on Dave's arm and said, "Please, Dave. I need some makeup and some fresh clothes. We just can't go on a voyage wearing these old tattered rags." There was pleading in her voice, and when she turned her large eyes on him, Dave immediately was swayed.

"Oh, well, I suppose it'll be all right. Come on then."

15

As Sarah walked along beside Josh, she noted that his lips were drawn tight with irritation. "Don't be mad at Dave, Josh," she whispered. "He'll be all right as soon as he gets used to being the leader. That's what he's always wanted to be, I suppose."

"Well, he's welcome to it," Josh snapped. "If he thinks he can do better than I can, more power to him!"

Sarah wanted to comment that Josh was behaving every bit as badly as Dave. She had learned, however, over the long months the two had spent together, that Josh was generally a sweet-tempered young man, terribly shy at times, and sensitive as a young girl. So what she said was, "Well, I guess we could use some supplies." She pulled at his patched shirt. "This shirt's so dirty you could stand it up in the corner!" Her eyes crinkled at him, and they laughed aloud.

"I guess so. Well, you get some nice things too. We can't go to these people looking like a troop of beggars, whoever they are." His brow wrinkled. "Goél wasn't very informative about them. He just said they were simple— but that could apply to almost any kind of folks. I guess we'll find out when we get there. Let's go—before Abigail buys the store out."

Sarah discovered to her delight that the shop was large and well-supplied, especially with gear intended for sailors.

"I don't want to buy any ships' compasses or things like that," Abbie said, "but look—they've got a nice stock of clothing. Let's go try some on, Sarah!"

"Oh, me!" Jake groaned, slapping his head in a forlorn gesture. "Once you get Abbie trying on clothes, that's it. We'll be lucky to get out of here a year from now!"

Jake's timing was off somewhat. But by the time the Sleepers had bought new clothes plus a few extras, it was late in the afternoon. The shopkeeper totaled up the bill, and Dave paid him out of the gold pieces that Goél had supplied.

The shopkeeper took the coins, weighed them carefully in his hand, then said, "Going on an ocean voyage, I take it! May a man ask where you're going?"

"We're going to a place called the Isle of Mordor," Dave replied.

"*Mordor!*" The man's eyes blinked with surprise—and something else.

Why—he looks scared out of his wits, Sarah thought.

The shopkeeper stared at the group of young people, then shook his head. "Well, good fortune be with you." But he sounded doubtful.

"Partner," Reb asked, "what's the matter with that place? You looked a little bit skeery when you heard the name."

The man clamped his lips together. He would say only, "I got nothing to say about the land of Mordor. Thank you kindly for your business."

"That's a strange thing," Sarah murmured as they left the shop. "I wonder what gave him such a scare?"

"Don't know," Josh replied. "One thing for sure—you wouldn't get *him* on a ship going to Mordor."

The Sleepers made their way down to the shore and looked at the boats anchored there.

"I don't know which one to go to first," Dave said, "but that's a nice-looking ship there."

The ship he indicated was the largest of the vessels bobbing at anchor. It had three masts and a comfortable width. On deck, sailors were mending sails, swabbing the deck, doing the things that sailors do when a ship is in port.

"I'll just go give them a hail," Dave said confidently.

As Dave walked toward the shore, Jake ambled over and said to Josh, "I can tell you one thing—this is not go-

17

ing to be a lucky voyage. Did you see the look on that shopkeeper's face when we mentioned the Isle of Mordor?" He shook his head dolefully. "I don't know what we're going into, but it's not going to be Disney World. There'll be something more there than a few rides. That's what I say."

They wandered up and down the beach until finally Dave's call drew them back. When they came up to him, he was looking highly satisfied.

"It's all taken care of," he said. "They'll drop us off on the Isle of Mordor, but it costs a pretty penny for our passage."

"Did the captain say anything about the place?" Sarah asked anxiously.

Dave's expression changed, but he merely said, "Well, he said it's a little off the beaten track, and he seemed surprised that we were going there. But he guaranteed to take us. And what's more, he said he'd bring his ship back to take us off. He passes by there on a regular basis."

Reb said, "When's he leaving? We've got to get our gear on board."

"First thing in the morning. He said if we could board tonight, he'd give us our quarters. So let's get our stuff loaded."

The next morning the ship sailed out of the harbor. There was much excitement among the Sleepers as they stood on deck watching the land disappear.

Abigail was wearing a new dress. It was a shade of light blue that matched her eyes and seemed very fragile after the rough clothing she had been wearing. She touched her hair and said, "I was glad that shop had some shampoo and some cosmetics. I don't feel ready for anything until I've done my face."

Reb grinned at the pretty girl. "Well, Abbie, you

done it up nice. Shucks—you look good enough to be buried right now! We wouldn't have to do a thing to you."

"Reb! What an awful thing to say!" But then Abigail laughed and put her arm through his. "Let's go to the front of this old boat. I've seen all I want to of that harbor. Let's see where we're going."

Dave watched them go. "I think that girl would flirt with a stone statue," he said. Still, he looked rather envious.

Sarah whispered to Josh, "I think Dave's jealous. He always did like Abigail." She looked up at him. "Just like you did. Remember the first time you saw her? I thought you'd fall over in a dead faint of admiration."

Josh blushed, but he said, "Aw, I didn't either. I'd rather have somebody with brains—like you—anytime, Sarah."

Somehow this compliment didn't please her, and she sniffed and drew away. "Come on, Jake, let's take a walk around the ship. We can talk to some of the sailors."

They had plenty of opportunities to talk to the sailors, for the voyage went on day after day. The food was good, and their sleeping accommodations were better than usual. After the long trek through the woods, a sea journey was a good time to rest up. They found the sailors jolly and very friendly. However they soon discovered that none of the mariners was willing to talk about the Isle of Mordor.

On the sixth day out, Josh and Sarah were sitting on kegs watching the cook, a small gnomelike figure named Bentley, who had, it seemed, traveled all over Nuworld. The pair had come to listen to his tales several times before.

Finally Josh said, "Look, Bentley, none of you on this ship will talk about the land of Mordor. What's wrong with it? Is there some kind of monster on it? Come on, level with me."

Bentley screwed his face into a scowl and scratched his sparse gray hair. "Well, now, lad," he said, "it's not the kind of place a man wants to talk about, if you catch my meaning."

"I *don't* catch it," Sarah replied instantly. "It must be a frightening place if you won't even talk about it. Have you ever actually been there, Bentley?"

The cook was peeling potatoes. He carefully pared away a long scrap, dropped it in a bucket, then tossed the potato onto a small mountain beside him.

"When I was a boy—no more than fourteen or fifteen, as I remember—I was on an old freighter. We hit a storm in those latitudes and had to put in. It tore the rigging out, so we had to stay until we got the sails repaired. Some of us had to go into the woods hunting for food. I went with them one time." He fell silent, picked up another potato, and began to peel it, his eyes moody. "There's *things* in that place."

"Things," Josh repeated. "What kind of things are you talking about? Wild animals?"

Bentley lifted his eyes. They were dark brown and deep-set. "Well, now, I'd seen wild animals afore, lad, but nothing like the things I saw there. Big things. Things like I ain't never seen since. Don't know how to talk about them. There's people in that place too—but they was crafty, they was. Two of our men got took."

"Got took?" Sarah asked in surprise. "What does that mean—'got took'?"

"I mean they just disappeared. Went off and never came back. We thought we heard them hollering once, and then it was cut off sudden, like someone had . . . had . . ." Then he snapped, "Don't like to think about those times."

"Is that all you can tell us?" Josh asked.

"Don't like to talk about it." Bentley had grown moody, and he said only, "Don't like to tell folks what to do, but you young folks are fools for going to the Isle of Mordor! People go there, and the funny thing is," he said, "they go in but most of the time they never come out again. Don't like to talk about it!" Then he turned his back on them.

Sarah and Josh went back on deck.

"He makes my flesh creep and shivers go up my back," Sarah said. "It's like going to a horror movie."

"It's worse than that," Josh agreed wryly. "It's the things I *don't* know that scare me. If you can see something, at least you know what it is you're afraid of—but the way all these sailors talk—even the captain—there's some things on the Isle of Mordor that must be awful."

"But we know there are people there that need our help," Sarah said. "So we've got to go, and that's all there is to it."

Two days later the ship docked in a little harbor. Reb and the other Sleepers were getting into a small boat for going ashore when Captain Shaw came to say good-bye.

"Good luck to you," he said rather grimly. "I'll stop off here the first of every month until I find out—" He broke off abruptly and then shook hands with them all. "Be careful now. Watch yourself, for that's a dangerous place. Wish you wouldn't go, but I see your mind's made up."

"Yes, we have to go, Captain Shaw," Dave said. "Be sure and check the shore for us. We'll be stuck here if you don't come and get us. Don't know how long we'll be, but it shouldn't be too long."

An hour later the Sleepers were standing on the beach, watching the sails of the ship grow smaller in the distance.

Everyone seemed reluctant to move, but finally Reb shrugged. "Well, she's gone. Let's get this here show on the road. Are you ready, Captain Dave?" He winked at Jake, for the two of them had given that name to Dave because he was so proud of his leadership position.

"Don't call me that!" Dave snapped. He pulled the map out of his pocket and stared at it. "Here," he said, "look at this."

They gathered around Goél's map. It showed a line of mountains and one large river running down to the ocean. "We'll have to follow the river. See, Goél has marked this area here—I guess that's the village where we're supposed to meet the people he's sending us to."

"Sure wish that river was going *up*, so we could just ride. We'll have to follow along the bank, I guess," Josh said. He looked at the sky. "It's about noon. You ready to start?"

Dave nodded and folded the map. "Yes. We'll find a camping spot before night so we can cook us a good meal. We'll have to do some hunting, though. The food we brought with us won't last very long. And we don't know what they'll have at the village. So let's go!"

They divided up the knapsacks containing their food, bedding, clothing, and equipment. The girls carried the smallest loads. They started walking along the east side of the river and soon discovered a path.

"Look here," Jake said, "this thing's been traveled. People must come from the village to the sea."

"That or animals," Reb guessed. "All animals like to go to water, but I guess it's probably both."

All afternoon they hiked. The jungle grew more dense as they made their way inward. Now huge trees towered overhead, sometimes shutting off the light of the sun and sometimes arching over the river from both sides until it was like walking down the aisle of a dim cathedral.

Late in the day Dave drew to a halt. "That's some nice ground over there and plenty of firewood. Let's camp here for the night."

"Suits me!" Reb said. "What do you want us to do, Captain Dave?"

Dave glared. "You can go gather firewood. You girls can get ready to cook a little something."

"What about you, Dave?" Josh inquired.

"I'm going to scout around—see what I can find out while the rest of you set up camp."

Dave walked farther upstream, and Wash said, "Well, we got our orders from Captain Dave. Let's get busy." He looked about at the towering trees. "Sure is quiet in here. I don't like it when it's too quiet. Makes me think something's ready to jump on me."

"Wash! Don't talk like that," Abbie said, shivering. "Let's get a fire built—a big one."

Soon they had a fire going and meat roasting on spits over it.

Dave came back, shaking his head. "Can't tell a thing about this place," he complained.

He sat down, took the meat Sarah offered him, and put it between two slices of bread. He waved the sandwich toward upstream. "This area turns into almost a swamp," he said. "I hope the path holds out. I went on a tour once in the Everglades. There were alligators and snakes and everything else." He shuddered. "I hate snakes!"

"So do I," Abigail said and moved closer to him. "What if we have to turn back?"

He looked at her in surprise. "That's the one thing we won't do. We've got to go on, no matter how hard it gets. If it gets too bad on land, we'll make a raft and pole our way up the river. It would be hard going, but we could do it."

"That's the way to talk, Dave," Josh said. "You're right—we've got to go on. Goél wouldn't be sending us on a foolish mission. It's important, whatever it is."

"What kind of people can they be, I wonder?" It had been a hard day, and Sarah was growing sleepy. "We've seen some strange varieties in our journeys—snakepeople, and giants, and dwarfs, and Gemini Twins." The thought of the twins they had encountered on their first adventure made her smile. "I wish Mat and Tam were with us now. They were a lot of fun."

Reb grinned. "You couldn't get them to go on a trip like this. They liked their comfort too much." He looked upriver. "I wish we had some hosses to ride. It'd sure beat walking through this old swamp. But we'll make it."

Jake looked around. "We've gotten real close, haven't we, the seven of us? Back in Oldworld we didn't even know each other, and now we're closer to each other than anybody else. I guess that's the way it is when you go on adventures with people. I hope we always stay close together."

His words reminded Sarah of the uncertainty of their future.

Finally Dave said, "We better roll up in our blankets. I want to get an early start tomorrow."

As usual the boys had brought along a small, lightweight tent for the girls. When the two of them had crawled into it and pulled up their blankets, Abbie said sleepily, "I wish we had a boat like we had back home. We could just get in it and go skimming up this old river. We'll never have that again, I don't suppose."

Sarah looked over at the girl's face. The light of the campfire flickered, and dimly she saw Abbie's beautiful features. She wished for the thousandth time that she had this girl's beauty, and she thought of Josh's remark. *I'd rather have someone smart—like you.* As she drifted off to sleep Sarah thought, *I'd trade all my smarts for Abbie's long eyelashes!*

Next day the Sleepers paused at noon to eat a brief meal, then continued along the riverbank. If anything, the trees grew larger and closer together here, so that the sky was simply closed off at times.

For three days they trekked. Fortunately the path was well worn. They were able to trap animals without any trouble—mostly rabbits, although something like a possum got into one of Reb's snares.

They carried no weapons, not even bow and arrows, for that had been one of Goél's instructions. Reb, however, had managed to form a slingshot out of a piece of elastic cord. He was a dead shot and could hit a target fifty feet away with such force it would bring down small game.

He came in one afternoon after a hunting trip and held up his bag. "Look what I got here!" he said, a smile on his face. When they gathered around, he said, "They *look* like squirrels, but look at the size of them! Why, these scamps—they're three times as big as any squirrels I ever saw in Arkansas!"

Josh held up one. "This thing is as big as a small dog. And look at the claws and teeth! Funny kind of squirrel."

"Well, we're gonna see if they're any good to eat!" Reb said. "Sure wish I had some dumplings. Nothing better than squirrel and dumplings. Save me some of the brains," he said, winking at Josh. "You ever eat squirrel brains, Abbie?"

"No!" Abbie shuddered. "And I'm not going to start either!"

They pressed on for another two days. Late the second afternoon, when they stopped for camp, Reb went out looking for game while the rest made a fire and set up the tent. He came back in less than ten minutes, a strange look on his face. "Better come and take a look at this," he said. "I ain't never seen nothing like it."

"What is it?" Dave asked.

But Reb only motioned for them to follow.

He paused at a cleared space beside the river and said, "Notice how the ground is kinda trampled? Well, look at this." He led them to the water and pointed to the ground.

Josh looked and said, "What is it? I don't see anything."

"Don't you see that track?" Reb demanded. "Look at it!"

Josh then saw that the track was so big he had missed it. It was at least a foot wide and more than three feet long. He had mistaken it for some sort of small crater.

Reb said, "He comes to the river to drink, whatever he is."

Josh stepped back, and the rest gathered around to stare.

Wash peered at the huge track and said, "Look at the claws on that critter's foot!" He shivered. "Whatever it is, I sure don't want to meet up with *him!*"

Dave frowned at the print. "I don't think *any* of us wants to see a thing like this—whatever it is."

"Bentley, the cook," Josh said. "Remember, he told us there were strange things on the Isle of Mordor. I don't like the looks of that."

"Let's get back to camp," Dave said. "*I* don't like being out in the open like this."

At the campsite, Wash said, "I think I'm gonna find me a different place to sleep tonight."

"Like where?" Dave demanded.

"Like up in a tree somewhere. *Way* up." He pointed at a tree where there were huge branches. "Maybe I'll climb up there and sleep."

"You'd fall out and break your neck," Dave said in disgust. "We'll be all right tonight. And we'll keep a sharp eye out tomorrow. We ought to be at the village in another two or three days."

But late that night Reb heard a strange thrashing about as if trees were being shoved aside, and Wash whispered, "You sure we don't want to go climb that tree, Reb? I don't want that big thing to come visiting."

"Aw, I'll pop him off with my slingshot." Later, however, he looked up at the tree and said, "Before this thing is over, we might all be up a tree, Wash."

3

The Lost World

I don't know how long we can keep going like this," Dave said, gazing out across the swamplike territory that stretched before them.

The Sleepers had been traveling for two days, and the going had been difficult. At times they had to wade through bogs where the mud sucked up around their ankles. They had seen little game on the way, so food was scarce.

Abbie sighed. "I wish we could get out of this mud. Look at me! I'm dirty from head to foot."

Wash piped up, saying, "I don't mind being dirty so much as I mind being hungry." He glanced about the swamp and then looked ahead. "That looks like a dry spot up there, Dave. Let's see if we can get out of this water."

The seven struggled on, their feet making sucking sounds as they pulled them free of the muck. But at last they found themselves up on dry and stony ground.

Wiping the mud off his boots as well as he could, Josh looked up at Dave. "What now? The river's getting smaller all the time."

"That's the way rivers do," Dave said nastily. "They're small where they start. I'm surprised you didn't know that, Josh." His tone was sharp.

Sarah thought Dave probably was unsure of himself and to cover this he asserted his authority. Seeing that Josh was about to answer back, she said quickly, "Let's go on. According to the map, we aren't too far away from the village." She stooped and washed her hands in the river, which was now more of a creek.

"All right," Dave said grudgingly. "I'd like to get where we're going. I'm tired of this trip. It's too much 'adventure' for me."

The land, Sarah saw, was broken up now by stony outcroppings. Here and there huge rocks began to appear, but the walking was much easier.

They had kept at it for more than an hour when Dave called a halt. "Let's stop here and rest. We'll spread out and see if we can find some game or something else to eat—maybe berries."

Sarah saw huge ferns and tall trees everywhere but nothing that looked like a berry bush.

"All right," Josh said doubtfully, "but it doesn't look very promising."

"I'll go with you, Josh," Sarah said, and the two of them walked off to the right.

As soon as they were out of hearing, Josh said angrily, "I don't see why Dave has to take everything out on me! He's just getting a swelled head. Besides, I don't think he knows what to do."

"Well, you know how that is, Josh. When we first got here and you were the leader, you were uncertain at times too. It's hard on Dave. Just be patient with him."

Josh grinned at her. "Always the peacemaker, aren't you? Well, I expect you're right. Come on, let's see if we can find something to eat."

But search as they might, they found nothing and finally returned to learn that the others, except for Wash, all had the same bad luck.

"Well," Dave said, "we can eat a little of this dried meat. Not much of it left, but it's—"

"Hey! Hey! Come and see what I've found!" Wash was standing on top of a large rock, waving wildly.

Dave motioned everyone to come. "Maybe he's found something to eat."

The Sleepers scrambled to their feet and ran to where the small black boy was almost jumping up and down with excitement. "Right over there! In that little crater!" Then Wash did jump up and down with excitement. "You—you're not going to believe this!"

He led them to a certain spot and pointed down. "How about that for lunch!"

The other Sleepers clustered around him.

Abigail gasped. "I never saw anything like that! What is it?"

"Why, it's eggs!" Wash said proudly. Leaning over, he touched one of six large, gray objects. "I don't know what kind of bird laid these things, but they're something, aren't they?"

Josh picked up one. It was larger than a bowling ball. He hefted it, his brow furrowing. "No bird laid these," he said. "There's never been a bird that big that I know of."

Dave said, "It has to be a bird. That's all that lays eggs."

"No," Josh said, "other things lay eggs. Big sea turtles, for example. But these aren't turtle eggs either. That only happens in the ocean."

"Well, what do you think it is?" Sarah asked.

Josh shook his head. "Don't know," he admitted. "Never saw anything like it." He looked down at the other eggs, neatly piled in a small pyramid. "And I don't know whether we'd want to eat them or not."

"Let's try one," Wash suggested. "Build up a fire, and we'll have the biggest omelet you ever saw in your whole life. I'm tired of stringy old rabbit meat!"

Quickly they built a fire, but when the girls had gotten out the skillets, Abigail said, "Dave, I don't know how to break one of those things. It's not like a hen's egg."

31

"Let me try," Jake offered and pulled out his pocket-knife. Using the butt end, he cracked one of the eggs at the top. "It's tough." Then he examined the rough, wrinkled shell. "I don't think we ought to eat this thing. We don't know what it is."

"Let me see," Dave said. He took the cracked egg and peered at the contents. Finally he too said, "No, we better not try this. We just don't know what it is." He straightened up and looked around. "I don't like this. I keep thinking about those stories the sailors told about this place—or didn't tell. They were too scared to talk about it. Let's get on our way."

The country changed again as they traveled that afternoon. They passed several hot springs that sent up spray and vapor. The massive boulders became as big as houses. The area now was a mixture of swampy places and rocky, arid land. At times they passed through huge forests of trees that none of them recognized.

At dusk they made camp again beside the river and ate most of their remaining provisions.

"We better find that village tomorrow," Reb said. "I don't fancy starving to death out here. Maybe we *could* catch a fish though." His brow furrowed. "Yeah, we can run us a trot line across the river."

"What's a trot line?" Abigail asked curiously.

"You don't know what a trot line is?" Reb was astounded. "You ain't been well brought up, Abbie. What you do is, you stretch a line across a creek about like this one here—or even a big river. Then you tie little lines with hooks about every five feet across it. You bait them up, and then you see what you get. You catch fish."

"We don't have a boat," Jake protested. "We don't have hooks."

"Shucks," Reb said, shrugging. "That river ain't very deep. Get some of that twine out. I'll put the line out while the rest of you make up some short lines. Make hooks out of that little bit of wire we bought."

They worked quickly, and within an hour they were ready. Reb waded across the stream—the water came up only to his chest. He tied one end of the line to a tree, then came back and said, "Now, give me them short lines."

"What you going to use for bait?" Josh inquired.

"Well, if there's any catfish in here, they'll eat just about anything. Use some of that dried meat—that'll do for a starter." When Abbie brought the remains of the meat, Reb started out again. He stopped at each hook and baited it.

When he returned, he said, "That's it! We ought to catch something. Now we'll wait about an hour, and then we'll run that line."

"Why do they call it a trot line?" Sarah asked.

"Because you put the line out in the river, build a fire up back a piece, and then every hour you trot down to the line and take the fish off," Reb explained.

They sat around the fire, waiting, hungry and uncomfortable. Mosquitoes began to hum in their ears, and finally, when it was almost dark, Reb said, "I reckon I'll go see if we got us a fish."

The rest, curious, followed to watch him.

Stepping into the stream, Reb walked out, lifting the line, and pulled up the first hook. "Nothing here! Hope we got better luck on them other hooks." He lifted up two more that were empty, then yelled, "We got one!"

The others watched excitedly as he lifted the line and they saw a fish flopping in the water. "Don't know what it is," he shouted, "but it's a good'n!" He started struggling to get the fish off the hook. "This thing's swallowed the hook. I don't know if I can get it off or not."

As Josh watched Reb tussle with the fish, a sudden movement across the stream caught his eye. He thought he saw something at the base of the trees. The others were so busy watching Reb that no one else seemed to notice anything.

Josh decided at first that his eyes were deceiving him. It was almost dark, and the trees cast long shadows. *I guess that was just a big boulder I saw, but*—he froze, for the "boulder" had moved! He squinted, and all of a sudden what he had thought was a boulder came into focus. Josh could not believe what he was seeing. A monstrous form was emerging from the forest and was headed for the river. It was so big he doubted his eyes, but he didn't doubt the long, sharp teeth.

A dinosaur!

"Reb, get out of there! Fast!"

Reb had just extracted the hook, and he straightened up, holding the fish. "What did you say?"

Josh screamed again, "Reb, look out!"

Reb looked behind him to where Josh was pointing, saw the beast, and he too froze.

Sarah and the others, after the first shock, now were yelling, "Run, Reb! Run! Come on!"

Reb dropped the fish and began splashing wildly back toward shore.

The dinosaur spotted him and plunged into the water.

To Josh, watching terrified, the creature looked at least twenty feet tall.

Splattering desperately, Reb reached the bank, then glanced back. The dinosaur was halfway across and wading swiftly.

"It's a Tyrannosaurus rex!" Jake yelled. "Let's get out of here!"

Reb stumbled up the bank and, running with all his might, caught up with the others.

Abigail tripped and fell, and Josh pulled her to her feet. He looked back, and the dinosaur was still coming, lifting its enormous feet in long strides. It had a mouthful of sharp teeth and front legs that seemed tiny compared to the rest of its massive body.

"Get in among the trees," Josh shouted. "We can hide there!" He motioned wildly, and the Sleepers raced to a grove of great trees packed so tightly together that they had to dodge around the trunks.

"This way!" Josh led them deeper into the forest. "Stay together. Don't get scattered." He held onto Abigail's arm.

She was weeping with fear.

He whispered, "Don't worry—we'll get out of this."

They ran until they could run no longer.

Somewhere far off sounded a crashing, but it grew fainter, and at last Dave said, "Whew! I guess he's gone."

Under the trees it was almost totally dark. Josh could barely see his friends' white, frightened faces. His voice was shaky as he said, "I guess now we know what happened to the people that disappeared on Mordor."

"There haven't been dinosaurs like that around for a long time back in Oldworld—but somehow they're in *this* world." Jake scrunched his eyes together, peering into the darkness. "That thing is one of the worst killers that ever walked the earth. It had teeth like chisels."

"We've got to go back," Abbie said and began to weep again. "We can't go on like this!"

"But we *can't* go back, Abbie," Dave said. His face was pale, but he seemed to remember that Goél said he was the leader. "Let's get back to camp. We're out of here in the morning. We'll stick to the trees. We'll get to the village, and then we'll be all right."

They almost tiptoed, returning to the campsite.

"What if that thing comes back tonight?" Wash asked when they arrived. "I wouldn't be more than a mouthful for that monster."

"We'd better move over among the trees," Dave said. "And we'll leave before daylight to get away from this place."

Jake said, "If we don't, we're liable to run into a t-rex again—or other things just as bad."

"What could be as bad as that?" Sarah shivered.

"Well," Jake said, "if there's one kind of dinosaur here, there's probably others. Some of them are a lot bigger than a t-rex, but some are smaller and faster. If it had been a velociraptor that had come after us, we'd be goners."

"Are they bigger than one of them rexes?" Reb asked.

"No. They weren't all that big, but they were quick. And they had talons like sickles on each foot. They could rip other dinosaurs to pieces."

"Let's hope we don't run into any of *those*," Dave said fervently. "Now come on. Let's move camp and wait for dawn."

Nobody slept well that night, and everyone arose with scratchy eyes and empty stomachs in the morning.

"Let's get the stuff together," Dave said. "I want to get out of this place."

The Sleepers spoke little as they continued along the river. Dave stopped once to check the map, then shook his head. "There are no landmarks, and I can't tell how many miles we still have to go. All I know is, the village is on up at the very head of this river."

Suddenly Abigail let out a scream. "Look! Look over there! In those trees!"

They all whirled. There, at some distance, something was moving.

The Sleepers were looking at a stand of very tall trees, but what was moving was no tree. Then a long neck stretched upward, and a head began to pull at the branches.

Dave stared at the creature's massive body, its elephantlike legs, and the long, serpentine neck. "What *is* it?"

"I know," Jake whispered. "That's a brachiosaurus. It's like one of the biggest dinosaurs that ever roamed the earth. That thing must weigh eighty tons."

The others seemed struck dumb by the sight. There was a whole herd of the monstrous beasts.

Jake said, "I read one time where dinosaurs like this stayed together in herds to protect themselves from the meat-eating dinosaurs like the T-rex."

"Are they dangerous?" Dave asked.

"Not like a T-rex. Of course, if one stepped on you, there'd be nothing left. But look how slow they move!"

They watched the huge beasts until Dave said nervously, "Let's get out of here before we see something worse."

The Seven Sleepers followed the river path for another two hours. Josh thought everyone seemed nervous now and tended to see something behind every tree.

At noon Dave called a halt again, and they threw themselves down under the shade of some huge ferns. "It can't be too much farther," he said. "And I sure don't want to stay out here another night."

"Me either," Reb said. "That dragon back in Camelot —I'd rather face that thing than one of them T-rexes. That's a bad critter, that is."

They rested for a time, but when Dave said wearily, "Time to go," they got to their feet and started down the trail once more. They were tired and hungry, and the mosquitoes had made a feast on them. But there was nothing to do but plod ahead.

Dave had just turned around to say, "Keep close now!" when Josh cried, *"Look out, Dave!"*

Dave whirled around, and everyone gasped.

Straight ahead down the path stood three men dressed in skins, their hair down to their shoulders—and each clutching a wicked-looking club with a stone for a head.

Dave held up a hand saying, "Greetings. We come from Goél. Peace be with you."

The three brutal-looking men did not speak or move.

Then a movement caught Josh's eye, and he saw several of the same kind of men appear from each side. He spun around. Two more had come up behind them, also carrying weapons and staring at the group with hard eyes.

"We're surrounded," Josh whispered. "What do they look like to you, Sarah?"

"They—they look like cavemen. Sort of like the pictures I've seen in books."

Reb looked around at the figures and said, "What they sure don't look like is friendly. I hope we haven't jumped out of the frying pan into the fire!"

4

A Welcome Visitor

One of the fierce men stepped closer. He was the tallest, was strong-looking, and was rather ferocious in appearance. He wore a single garment made of some sort of brown fur with a hole for his head, leaving his arms free. He had black eyes, as they all appeared to have, and clutched his war club. Holding it high, he said, "You come to Mordor."

Dave was relieved. He had worried about whether the inhabitants of this strange land would speak a language he could understand. The man's speech seemed to be a simplified form of common Nuworld dialect, understood almost anywhere.

Dave lifted his hand again in a peaceful gesture. Speaking slowly he said, "We come from Goél to help your people."

The man struck his chest with his free fist. "Lom!" he said, apparently giving his name. "Warrior." Then his eyes glittered with a strange sort of look. "You come Mordor to kill us!"

Dave was alarmed and shook his head. "No!" he cried. "We come to do you good." He spread his hands wide in a pleading gesture. "We are from Goél."

Lom stared at him. "I know no Goél," he said. He came forward with raised ax until he stood no more than two feet from Dave. Slowly he reached out and plucked at Dave's shirt curiously. Then he looked up. "You come spy! You not good people."

Another warrior joined him, a squat, muscular man. He suddenly grabbed Sarah's hair.

She let out a scream.

Reb jumped to help her. He was knocked flat on his back by a blow from the squatty man, who laughed roughly and said, "You fight me? I kill."

He lifted his ax, and a cry of alarm went up from the Sleepers.

"Wait!" Dave yelled, standing over Reb and holding up both hands. "He meant no harm. Don't hurt him!"

Lom stared at him hard. Suspicion was still in his dark eyes, but he finally seemed to make a decision. "You come," he grunted. When they hesitated, he brandished his weapon. "Come!" he repeated loudly, and the rest of the dangerous-looking band moved in closer.

"Come on," Dave said quickly. "We'll go with them."

The Sleepers found themselves herded like sheep. From time to time Lom would call out something to the other members of his party. But when the Sleepers tried to speak, one of the band would shout and wave his ax.

Their captors were obviously in better condition than the Sleepers, for the young people were soon gasping for breath. Lom led them into jungle and across streams, and once Josh muttered, "They must have feet like iron! They're stepping on sharp rocks that hurt me even through my boots."

Josh and Sarah were in the middle of the line, and at the moment none of their captors seemed to be watching.

"What kind of people *are* they?" murmured Sarah.

Josh glanced around at the men and shook his head. "I don't know. I thought at first they looked like what cavemen were supposed to look like. But they're not. I mean, all the pictures of cavemen make them have stupid-looking faces, foreheads sloping back, and big jaws. These

40

fellows look about like us except they've got more hair and are a lot stronger."

But he had no time to say more, for Lom turned and saw them talking. He came back and seized Josh by the arm with a grip that made the young man wince. It was like being grabbed by steel pincers.

"No talk," Lom threatened. He slapped the flat of his ax against Josh's head. It was a light tap, but it made Josh see stars. "No talk!" Lom repeated and then returned to the head of the line.

Josh ignored the pain in his head and nodded to show Sarah that he was all right.

After what seemed like forever, Lom called a halt. The Sleepers at once sat down, gasping for breath.

Lom said to some of his men, "Go see." These fanned out, leaving only Lom and four men to watch the Sleepers.

Dave tried to talk to one of the young guards. "What are you going to do with us?" When he got no answer, he said, "Take us to the head man of your village. What's his name?"

Lom was watching them with a curious expression. "No. You come for spy on The People," he said. When Dave shook his head, Lom spoke louder. "We give you to Greska."

"Greska?" Dave asked, a puzzled look on his face. "Who is Greska? Is he one of your people?"

"No! Not people."

"Does he belong to one of the tribes close by?"

"No!"

Dave was bewildered. "Well, who *is* Greska?"

Lom swept his hand around toward the sky. "Greska, big. Strong, very strong."

"I think he means he's a god," Jake spoke up.

41

A frightening thought occurred to Dave. "What do you mean, Lom—you're going to give us to Greska?"

The young man had a firm mouth. He was nice looking in a way, but there was an ugly light in his eyes. He grunted. "We give you to Greska." He raised his club in a threatening gesture, struck the ground with it, then pointed at Dave's head. "Tomorrow morning we give you to Greska."

That night the Seven Sleepers were herded into a small holding area. They huddled together and made no attempt to put up the tent for the girls. Two hunters kept a close watch on them. Lom himself watched for a time, then left. The young people curled up, ready to try to sleep.

The guards too appeared sleepy, and Dave finally risked saying, "It doesn't look good. I never thought we'd wind up as human sacrifices."

"Maybe you misunderstood him," Josh said. "He doesn't talk very plainly."

"I could tell what he meant." He swallowed hard. "I'd give a lot to see Goél come walking out of those woods."

Sarah had been sitting with knees up, her face resting on her arms. Now she looked up, and the stars that sparkled overhead and the full moon lighted her face, making it silver. "We've been in tight places before," she said quietly. "Goél won't let us down. He never does."

"Dog my cats!" whispered Reb. "If you ain't a fine one, Sarah. Always got an encouraging word. We shore need one, I'd say." He looked at the guards. "These fellows are stronger than snuff. I wish we had some hosses and could gallop right back where we come from—or at least get on to the village."

They lay whispering for a time. Then, hungry and tired and scared, they finally dozed off.

Josh awoke to the sound of stirring. Then he saw

Abigail looking around with a frightened expression.

She turned to Dave. "What are we going to do?" she whispered.

"I don't guess we're going to do anything," Dave muttered.

He stood up, for Lom appeared from behind a stand of trees and was approaching. He held his ax in his hand, and he suddenly swept his free hand toward the sun, just rising and casting an orange glow over the earth.

"Greska hungry," he said.

"Greska must be the sun," Josh whispered to Sarah. "They are sun worshipers of some kind."

Dave swallowed and said to Lom, "Please let us talk to your chief."

But the young man looked fearfully toward the rising sun. Josh suddenly understood that somehow Lom had gotten into his head that it would please his god, Greska, if they were sacrificed.

And although Dave talked long and hard, Lom made no further answer.

At last the warrior waved his men into a tighter circle. "We give spies to Greska," he said and raised his ax.

Josh looked around and saw the eyes of the men glinting. *They look like wolves around a helpless victim,* he thought. Then he took Sarah's hand. "No matter what happens," he whispered, "I want you to know you're the finest girl I've ever known."

Sarah gave his hand a squeeze but seemingly was unable to speak.

Now the rays of the sun threw a reddish glow on the Sleepers, and Dave said suddenly, "Sorry I led you into this. I should have done better."

"Oh, shoot," Reb said. His face was pale, making his freckles stand out, but he managed a grin. "Couldn't nobody done better, Dave. Don't you worry about it." He turned to Wash then and said, "Good buddy, we've had some times, haven't we? If this is it, I want you to know I ain't never had a better partner."

The black boy swallowed hard and looked into the eyes of the friends surrounding him, but could not say a word.

Lom slowly raised his ax higher, and Wash whispered, "Guess this is it."

But at that moment, when all the warriors were closing in with upraised axes, another voice suddenly broke the silence.

"Lom!"

The leader turned, and every Sleeper turned, to see who had spoken.

It was a young girl. She had dark hair, and her skin was tanned a beautiful golden color. She wore a white fur garment that left her arms free and fell shortly above her knees. She carried no weapons, but there was some sort of pouch across her shoulder and a red stone dangled about her neck from a leather thong.

"Eena," Lom said. He nodded toward the Sleepers. "We catch spies. Give to Greska."

A ray of hope came to Josh, for the girl's face was not hard. She had a curious look in her dark eyes though, and she stood beside Lom, staring at them.

"We are friends," Dave said quickly. "We come to do good to your people, Eena."

The girl seemed surprised at the use of her name. She turned to Lom. "Where you find these people?"

"Down by river. We give to Greska."

Time seemed to stop for Josh. The Sleepers had been in many dangerous situations but never one like this. It seemed as though they were on a thin wire, and a breath could blow them off. For if this girl agreed with the young man, they were all doomed. Josh held his breath and squeezed Sarah's hand.

"No," the girl said. "We take to cave."

Anger crossed the warrior's face, and he shook his head. "No! Give to Greska!" he insisted.

The others muttered agreement, but the girl did not appear to be troubled.

"Please, we mean no harm," Sarah said, stepping toward Eena. "Just let us talk to your chief."

The girl seemed interested in Sarah, and she came closer. As if she were touching a tree or a stone, she ran her hand down Sarah's smooth cheek. She pulled off Sarah's hat and looked at her hair, braided the way Sarah often wore it. She took one of the braids, gave it a pull, and then laughed. "Your hair funny." Then she felt the dark-blue cotton shirt Sarah was wearing, and Sarah stood very still.

Josh was watching the faces of the men and saw that they were angry but were keeping their eyes fixed on the girl. *She must be somebody important.*

Even as the thought crossed his mind, Eena said, "We go to Clag."

"Who is Clag?" Dave asked quickly.

"Clag, chief." Eena looked at him and nodded. "He my father." She ignored the mumbles and grumbles of the men, saying, "Go, Lom."

The young hunter whirled and strode down the path.

The Sleepers let out a collective sigh.

Reb said, "Boy, you couldn't get no closer to trouble than that, could you, Wash?"

The small boy's eyes were big as saucers. "I don't know who that Eena is, but she kinda reminds me of John Wayne coming with the cavalry to save the wagon train."

"Yep! I reckon that's what she is." Reb appraised the girl. "Didn't expect to see a fine-looking lady like that, did you, Abbie?"

45

Abbie was looking at Eena too, envy in her eyes. "If she would go get her hair done and take more care with her nails, she might be presentable," she said stiffly.

"Why, she looks good to me like she is," Reb protested, "but I wouldn't care if she was ugly as a pan of worms. She got us out of this mess."

"It's not over yet," Josh warned. "Her father—this Clag—might want to give us to Greska too." He looked at the girl. "I hope she's got some influence with her dad. We're sure resting in her hands."

The party traveled quickly down the trail. At one point Jake shouted, "Look up there! That's one of those pterodactyls. Never thought I'd see one of them."

Dave saw overhead a huge, batlike creature with widespread, leathery wings, a long tail, and a long beak full of sharp teeth.

"Well, he ain't no robin, is he?" Reb said. "He looks like he could eat a coon with them sharp teeth of his."

The Sleepers watched the strange creature sail by.

Eena was walking beside Dave. "You come from other place?"

"Yes, far away. Across the sea."

"Across big water? We never go there. Bad place."

Dave smiled, thinking of the stories of the sailors. "People there think *this* is a bad place."

"No," Eena said with surprise.

She looked up at him, and he noticed how large and clear her eyes were and how smooth her skin.

"This *good* place," she said.

"But Lom was going to kill us all. *That's* not good."

"Good to kill bad people," Eena said simply.

She said it casually, and Dave was shocked at a young girl's speaking of killing so lightly.

46

Then she looked at him again, studying his face. "I no think you bad."

Dave grinned, feeling encouraged. "I hope your father doesn't think so."

By the time they reached the village, he had gotten better acquainted with the girl. She asked him many questions in her broken speech about where they came from. Finally they came around a turn in the river, and he saw a line of high bluffs.

"There home," Eena said, pointing.

He saw some dark openings high in the cliff. They could be reached only by climbing what looked to be a narrow, precarious path, and he knew at once that the people had sought shelter from the fierce beasts that must roam the plains.

"Come," Eena said.

Ten minutes later they arrived at the foot of the cliff, where they were met by a crowd of staring men, women, and children. They babbled with excitement, and a thickset man with gray streaking his black hair came up to look at them.

"Who these people?" he demanded.

"They spies," Lom cried. "Come do wrong. I give to Greska." Then he cast an angry look at the girl. "Eena say 'No, bring here.'"

Eena went up to the man. "These not bad people. They good."

She turned to the Sleepers. "This my father. Chief Clag. You talk him now," she said to Dave.

Dave bowed and then held his palms outward to show he had no weapon. "Your daughter is right, Chief Clag. We come from a long way. We are sent by a good being named Goél. He sends us to help you."

Clag listened, and then he looked at his daughter thoughtfully. He was a short man but muscular. He had a

47

large head and appeared to be very strong. Like the others, he wore fur garments and carried a war club with a flint head.

Then he nodded. "We talk." He turned to the woman standing behind him and said, "We eat."

A sigh of relief went through Dave, and he turned to the other Sleepers. "Well, it looks like we've made it this far. Let's hope that Lom doesn't get any more big ideas."

Sarah came up, smiling. "Somehow I think Goél's been with us, but you did fine, Dave. Just fine."

He flushed and shrugged. "I can't take any credit. If it hadn't been for Eena, I think we'd all be dead by now." He looked at the girl, who now began leading them along the small ledge pathway that led upward to the caves. "She's some girl, isn't she?"

Sarah smiled again. "Yes, she sure is. She's some girl, Dave!"

5
No Room for Kindness

The Sleepers learned that the members of the tribe referred to themselves as The People—as though they were the only people on the face of the earth.

"A pretty narrow view, isn't it?" Dave muttered when Josh gave him this information. "Pretty egotistical, if you ask me."

"I think that's not unusual though," Josh said. "Some of the American Indian tribes—the Sioux, I think—thought the same thing. And others."

"Look!" Wash said. "I think it's time to eat. Let's go see if we can behave ourselves at their dinner table."

They had entered the main cave, a gigantic natural formation.

"They never dug *this* one out with their little hatchets," Reb said. "It'd taken them a million years." He stared about the cavern. It was at least twenty feet high and probably forty feet wide at the broadest point. "I guess they all live together in here."

A fire blazed in the cave opening, and some women were roasting meat on sharp sticks. Since the smoke had no way to escape except through the entrance, it filled the air, and Abigail fell to coughing.

Sarah slapped her on the back. "Don't let them see that you're offended, whatever you do."

Then Sarah moved over to Josh. "What do you think that meat is?" She shuddered. "I hope it's not something horrible."

"Well, whatever it is, let's try to make the best of it," Josh said. "Look, I think the chief's winding himself up for a speech."

Chief Clag stood before the fire and addressed the Sleepers. In essence, what he said was that they were on trial. If they proved themselves honest and honorable, they would be welcome. If they did not, they would be offered up to Greska. After Clag had finished reporting this cheerful news, he turned to Dave and grunted, "You talk."

Dave swallowed, and Wash patted him on the back. "Go on, Dave. You tell 'em."

Dave bowed to the chief and then began to speak. He said, "Chief Clag, and all of you members of The People, we thank you for allowing us into your home. We thank you for your hospitality."

Actually he thought he was making a rather good speech. But he saw them scratching their heads and realized he would have to speak much more simply. "Thank you for the meat that I suppose you are going to share with us." He thanked them for everything he could think of and finally bowed again and stepped back.

Wash whacked him on the shoulder and said, "You done fine, brother, just fine!"

Then the Sleepers were given their first meal, which proved to be an education. They soon discovered that there was no such thing as a "dinner table."

The meal began when Clag gave a sharp command and the women came forward. Not only were there no tables, there were no plates, no knives, no forks. Each member of The People snatched his chunk of meat off one of the sharpened sticks and fell back, gnawing at it, casting his eyes around like a dog afraid someone would steal his meal.

Abigail received her portion gingerly, took a bite of it in despair, and chewed. "I suppose it's something horrible," she said, "but actually it doesn't taste too bad."

"What does it taste like to you, Reb?" Josh asked the tall Southerner.

Reb was chomping thoughtfully. "Well, mostly I guess it tastes like hawk."

"*Hawk!* What does *that* taste like?"

"Hawk? Why, I guess it tastes a little bit like fox."

Josh threw up his hands. "Whatever we're eating now won't be as bad as eating a fox."

Reb grinned. "Rightly, it tastes a little bit like possum. Not quite as greasy though. Ain't bad, is it?"

Abigail had been watching The People eat, and she said angrily, "Look at that! The women and children! They get what's left over, and there's not much. I'd like to tell those men a thing or two."

"Wait a minute, Abbie," Dave cried in alarm. "Don't get anything stirred up. Remember what Goél said—we're supposed to do things slowly, not interfere with their habits."

"All right," Abbie said grimly, "but sooner or later, we're going to do something about *that!*"

After the meal was finished, Dave sat down beside Eena.

She smiled at him.

And then Dave noticed Lom, seated across the cave with his back against the wall, scowling at him. "Is that your boyfriend, Eena?"

"Boyfriend? What a boyfriend?"

Dave never had so much trouble trying to explain a simple expression. When he had finally finished, Eena said, "No, he not my mate."

"I didn't exactly mean that."

"Maybe he like to be," Eena said with satisfaction. Then she gave Dave another smile, "You want fight him for me?"

Dave took one look at the deadly looking ax that lay at Lom's feet and said quickly, "No, no, I don't think I'd like to do that!"

"You no think I nice?"

Then Dave spent the next five minutes trying to patch up his mistake. He managed somehow to convince the young girl that she was *very* nice but that he did not want to offend Lom, therefore he would not fight him for her.

Eena seemed not quite satisfied, but she said, "Come, I show you something."

Dave followed her across the cavern to where she paused before a young man with brown hair and mild brown eyes.

"Come, Beno," she commanded.

The young man got up at once. As they left the cave, Dave saw that he limped. His right leg was twisted, and his foot would not meet the floor easily.

The three walked down the ledge to a much smaller cave, not more than ten feet square. They stepped inside, and Eena said, "This Beno's cave. Show him, Beno."

The young man, who was apparently very shy, straddled a log and picked up what appeared to be a small stone. With the other hand he pulled from his pocket a larger rock with sharp edges. He put the small stone on the log, aimed carefully, and struck it a sharp blow. A flake of stone fell off. He struck again and again, and all of a sudden Dave understood.

"Why, he's making an ax head—out of flint."

"Yes. Beno only one among People who can do. You try?"

Dave was fairly clever with his hands so he agreed at once. Sitting down, he held the stone Beno gave him, gripped the larger rock, and took careful aim. He struck, but it was his own finger that he hit.

"Ow!" He dropped both stones.

Eena and Beno laughed, and for a moment he stared at them angrily. Then he joined in, saying, "I guess I'll leave the ax-head making to you, Beno. It's very good work. How do you know where to hit it?"

The young man shrugged. "I just know."

"He make many things, all good," Eena said proudly. "Now I show you something."

They left Beno behind in the cave, and as they walked down toward a clearing, Dave said, "It's a shame he's crippled."

"What is 'crippled'?"

"I mean, he can't walk very well."

"No. Fell from big cave when he little. Never walk good since."

They reached what appeared to be a small field of tall grass. Eena looked up at him proudly. "This mine!"

"This field is yours?"

"Field belong nobody. *This* mine!" She reached down and plucked up a stalk of the grass.

He saw now that it was some sort of grain. He looked over the field and understood. "You mean you grew this?"

"Yes. Here, you eat." She stripped off a handful of the heads, poured them into his palm, and did the same for herself. "Eat," she said. "Very good."

The grain had a slightly dusty taste but a rather pleasant, nutty flavor. He almost strangled when he tried to swallow but managed to get it down. "Very good," he agreed.

"Start little." She made a sign with her hand. "Long time ago. Every year I scatter more. Now, big field."

Actually it was a rather small field, but Dave saw the potential. "I think I can show you how to make this a lot better to eat, Eena. We'll have a regular bread factory, if you'll just give me time."

"What 'bread'?" she asked, a puzzled look on her face.

"I'll have to show you."

As they climbed back to the large cave, she said, "Tribe no like grass. They say better eat meat. But sometimes meat hard to find. Grass always good, even when put in cave for long time."

Dave stared at her with admiration. "You're probably the first farmer in Nuworld." Then, recognizing that she did not know what a farmer was, he said, "I can help you with this, Eena, and it'll be a good thing for your people."

By the time they got back, it was growing dark. Dave joined the other Sleepers, who formed a little island at one side of the cave. While they sat talking, he studied The People and noticed that they kept looking fearfully at the cave opening.

Josh said, "What's wrong with them? They look afraid."

"I think they're afraid of the dark."

"I don't blame them for *that!*" Abigail shuddered. "With those T-rexes outside and no telling what else, it's something to be afraid of."

"I guess that's why they live in this cave up here. A T-rex couldn't get up that cliff—or any of those dinosaurs." Jake nodded. "Pretty smart."

As time passed and the darkness became complete, the cave was lit by only the flickering fire.

Suddenly an old man got up and stalked to the cave mouth. He was wearing bracelets made of bone, and his face was painted.

"I hadn't noticed him before, but I bet I know what he is," Sarah said.

"What?" Josh demanded.

"I bet he's their witch doctor. My parents used to say every tribe back in Oldworld had a witch doctor of some kind."

Her words seemed to be true. The old man began to dance around, uttering strange sounds. His chant grew shriller as time went on, and then the witch doctor walked back and forth before the frightened members of the tribe, shaking a sort of rattle in their faces.

He chanted of the horrible things that lay outside in the dark that only he and Greska, the sun god, could save them from.

Moans of fear went over The People, and children buried their faces against their mothers' sides. Even the strong warriors had nothing to say but sat with lips clenched.

At last the weird old man came to the Sleepers, and an evil light shone in his eyes. He shook his rattle in Jake's face and renewed his chant.

Jake looked around with a frightened expression himself. "What's he doing anyway?"

And then the medicine man—his name was Grak, Eena said—shouted, "Feed to Greska! Make Greska happy!"

"This sounds like the same thing we heard before," Dave said in alarm, but before he could say more, Lom and another young man leaped up and seized Jake by his arms.

Grak snatched up a war club and raised it as though to bash Jake's brains out.

Dave scrambled to his feet, but Eena's voice stopped him.

"*Father!*"

Clag at once said, "No! No! No food for Greska."

Grak screamed, but the chief was adamant. "They no be killed. Not yet," he said firmly. There was a fierce struggle of will between Grak and Clag, but it was the chief who won out. He lifted his ax and motioned toward the small, wizened figure of Grak. "No." Then he turned around and said, "People sleep now."

Jake's face was pale. "That was a close one. We'll have to watch our step around here."

"You're right about that!" Wash agreed. "That old guy's mean clear through. I've seen lots of folks like him."

"Well, I don't guess we're going to be shown to our room in the Holiday Inn," Dave said. "Looks like we better just roll up right here." He saw that all the tribespeople had fur robes. "And they're not offering us any of those, so it'll be blankets for us."

The People watched as the Sleepers pulled blankets from their backpacks, and there was a babble of voices as though they had done something magical.

Abigail and Sarah were arranging their sleeping spot when Abbie said, "What's that man looking at you for?" She indicated a hairy, short, stocky individual who had been staring intently at Sarah.

"He's been looking at me like that ever since we came," Sarah muttered. "I wish he'd look at somebody else."

Abigail shuddered. "I wouldn't be surprised but what he's thinking about offering to buy you. That seems to be the way they do things around here. I feel sorry for the women and children."

"Yes, they need kindness," Sarah answered.

Abigail let the silence run on, interrupted now and then by the sounds of a crying child and the shuffling of the old woman who kept the fire going. Then she said, "I don't guess there's much room for kindness. Not in this world."

"I think that's why Goél sent us here—to show a little kindness."

6
Bakery

Clag summoned all the boys to go on a hunting trip. The girls, of course, stayed behind, and the first thing Abbie demanded was a bath. She sought out Eena.

"Eena, I need to take a bath."

"A bath? What a bath?"

Abbie tried to explain, but the concept was too difficult for Eena.

Sarah, who had been listening, smiled and said, "I guess one picture is worth a thousand words, Abbie. Come along—let's go down to the river."

They put a change of clothes and some soap into Abbie's backpack, then made their way with Eena down the cliff, through the field, and to the stream. After Abbie and Sarah had bathed and washed their hair, they dressed and spread their hair out to the sun, which was beginning to grow warm.

Abbie had brought along her new cosmetic case and now began to apply makeup.

Eena's eyes grew wide as she watched the process.

Abbie turned and said, "You are a very pretty girl, Eena. Would you like to try some of this?" She extended the lipstick and the small mirror.

Eena took the lipstick in one hand and the mirror in the other, obviously not knowing what to do next. Then she turned the mirror toward her face. When she saw her image, she gave a little scream, dropped both objects, and jumped to her feet.

Sarah scrambled up and put her arms around her. "It's all right, Eena. It's not magic. Look!" She held the mirror, put the girl's hand on the surface, and said, "You've looked in the river or in a pond and seen yourself, haven't you? Well, this is almost the same."

After some time she got the girl quieted.

Then Eena became very interested. She touched the lipstick with a finger and smeared color on her mouth. Then she looked in the mirror and nodded. "Good!" she said.

Abbie was amused. "Let me help you with that." She began putting a little makeup on Eena's face. As she worked, she said, "I think Lom likes you a lot."

"Yes. Want me for mate."

Sarah, who had been watching the young man Beno, said, "Beno is very nice."

"Yes, Beno good," Eena answered, "but he no bring home food."

"But he makes the clubs that they kill the game with," Sarah said.

But this concept seemed far beyond Eena.

Then a thought came to Sarah. "Eena, if the men don't bring back something to eat, you go hungry, don't you—the whole tribe?"

"Yes, men must bring food."

Sarah's face grew thoughtful. She tapped her lower lip, then said, "I want to show you something, Eena. A way you can have something to eat even if the men don't kill any animals."

Eena stared at her unbelievingly.

"Dave told me about the field where you grow grain. Would you show it to me?"

"Yes, I show."

Sarah and Abbie gathered their things and followed her to the small grainfield. "It was very wise of you to grow this," Sarah said. "Would you let me show you how to cook it?"

Eena looked bewildered.

"I'll show you. You and Abbie gather some of this grain. Abbie, why don't you put it in the backpack, and I'll go back and start preparations. We're going to start a bakery school today."

As Abbie and Eena began to gather the ripe grain into the bag, Sarah went back toward the cave. She knew that the grain would have to be ground into flour, so on the way she searched for just the right rocks to perform that operation. She finally found a large concave stone with a natural hole worn in it, perhaps by water, and then looked for a rounded one that would fit inside.

Having found that, Sarah began hunting for flat rocks. Fortunately there were many of those around, and she built what amounted to a small oven. She could think of no way to build a door, but she was confident that her stone oven would bake bread.

Eena and Abbie soon returned with a bagful of grain.

"That's fine," Sarah said. "Now, let me show you how to do this." She put a handful into the concave rock. Then, taking the rounded stone, she began to pound the grain. When she finished she had crushed it into a kind of rough flour. It was more like cornmeal, but she knew it would do.

Scooping some up, she put it into one of the pans they had carried for cooking stew.

"Now, you try it, Eena."

As Eena began to pound the grain, Sarah noticed that the women and children had gathered around them. "This is what we call making bread," she said. She tried to explain the process, but it seemed beyond their ability to understand. "I wish we had some milk," she said, "but water will have to do."

A small boy—Tor, his name was—asked her what milk was. When she explained awkwardly, his face lit up. "Come, you see."

Mystified, Sarah followed him, and not far from the cave she found a goat and a small kid. They bleated, and the boy said, "Milk!"

"That's wonderful!" She went back for a stone container and soon had milked the goat. "I learned how to do this on my grandfather's farm," she told Tor as she finished. "Now, we'll make something good to eat."

By the time she got back, she found that Abbie and Eena had ground enough meal to make a small supply of bread.

Sarah began to mix the milk and the flour, adding some salt from their own supplies. She showed the women how to make small round cakes. "You do it like this," she said.

Soon the women were all eager to try their hand at it.

When the little cakes were made, Sarah put them on the flat rock inside the oven. "Now we build a fire and let them cook. Tor, will you make a fire in front of this little house?"

She motioned to the stone structure, and Tor at once began to gather sticks. Then he brought a glowing branch from the fire in the big cave and soon had a brisk blaze going in front of Sarah's oven.

As the cakes cooked, Sarah and Abbie talked with the women. They had become very friendiy and seemed interested in everything about the two strange girls. From time to time they would reach out and touch their long, silky hair, seemingly mystified by it. Their clothes fascinated them too, especially their shoes.

Finally the cakes were done. Sarah reached in with a stick and awkwardly pulled one out. "I wish we had some yeast," she said to Abbie. "This is what they called 'unleavened bread,' I guess. Somehow we'll find some kind of yeast, and then we can have real biscuits."

She took the first cake, broke it in two, and handed half to Eena and the other half to Tor. "Taste it and see if it's good."

Both the boy and the girl looked at the bread doubtfully. Then each took a bite.

"Oh, hot!" Tor touched his tongue. But soon he bit off a chunk and began to chew. An odd expression crossed both his face and Eena's.

"Good!" she said and chewed eagerly. "Bread—good!"

The rest of the women crowded around. There was not enough for all to sample, but they made bread three times that day.

As they sat in front of the oven, waiting for the last batch to bake, Eena said, "Now, we have food even when men no get game."

When the hunters came back, they brought only one small creature that looked like an undersized antelope, not nearly enough to feed the whole tribe.

Eena ran to her father, holding up a cake and saying, "Eat."

Clag stared at her, took the morsel of rounded bread, and took a bite out of it. He was obviously hungry after his long hunt, and as he ate she explained to him how it had been made from the grass that grew in her field.

"See, we plant big field. Put grain in cave. When we hungry, we cook."

An odd look crossed Clag's face. Clearly he had never had such a concept before this. As far back as any man of The People could remember, if they did not find meat they starved. He stared at Eena, then at the two girls. "Good. What you call this?" When they told him, he repeated the word. "Bread, good. We have bread."

Dave came over to the girls and smiled. "It looks like you had a better day than we did. I'm glad you thought of this." Then he said, "Eena, it looks like you're going to be the farmer in this tribe." He had to explain again what a farmer was, and she seemed pleased with the idea.

But one was not pleased. Lom had a scowl on his face. When he was offered a bit of the bread, he tasted it and spit it out and said, "No good. Need meat."

Dave tried to make peace with the young man. "It doesn't mean you won't have meat," he said, "but when you have a bad hunting day—like we did today—it's nice to have something to eat, isn't it?"

Lom was insulted. "Me hunter—best hunter in tribe. I bring home meat." He saw that the others were watching, and he said defiantly, "Greska angry. When Greska no angry, we kill meat again."

A thought suddenly seemed to come to Lom. "We *have* meat." He looked to his right, and a smile touched his lips. "We kill goat."

The little boy Tor cried, "Don't kill the little one, Lom."

But Lom was angry and said, "We have meat. Kill both."

He stomped off, and the boy's face screwed up as if he would cry. "He kill goat, Eena?"

Eena said, "Lom catch goat. It his. He do what he want."

But Dave had heard the conversation. He ran after Lom. "Lom, let me talk to the chief, please."

Clag was not far away and, overhearing, turned toward them.

"Chief," Dave said, "I know you're hungry and the goat would be good eating. But think about this—there may be a time when you're even hungrier. Wouldn't it be good to have meat *then?*"

62

"Hungry now." Clag shook his head. "Lom catch goat. It his."

Dave turned back to Lom. "Then think about this—if we could capture a male goat and keep the male and female together, they'd have little goats like this one. Soon you might have many little goats. Then, every time you get hungry, you could kill a goat and have food. Besides—" he looked at Sarah "—it takes milk to make good bread, doesn't it, Sarah?"

When she nodded, he went on. "So if you keep a flock of goats you'd have milk and meat when you wanted it. You wouldn't have to depend on luck in hunting."

But Dave saw that he was wasting his breath.

Lom's face was set in an angry expression. He glared at Dave and said, "We eat *now!*"

Dave came back and put his hand on Tor's shoulder. "Sorry 'bout that, Tor—I did the best I could."

"Yes, you did, Dave," Jake said. "Like a fellow once said, if somebody don't want to do something, you can't make him."

Lom butchered both the goat and the kid, and the tribe ate.

Later on, after the meal, Eena came over and sat down close to Dave. "I wish Lom no kill goat." She sighed. "Now we no have milk for bread."

"Don't worry." Without thinking, he reached over and patted her hand. "We'll go catch another goat. I don't think it'll be too hard. Then I'll give it to you. It'll be yours to do with what you want."

Eena looked up at him, and a smile came over her face. Then she looked down at his hand on hers and slowly lay her other hand over his, capturing it. "I like you much," she said. "You good."

Dave felt his face flush. And then he glanced up to see that Lom was watching. He pulled his hand back quickly and tried to laugh. "Where I come from, guys don't give girls goats as presents—but I guess this is a special kind of place."

7

A Case of Hero Worship

You know, Wash, it don't seem like we've been here as long as we have," Reb said. "How long has it been now? Three weeks?"

Wash looked up from the mass of small vines that he was weaving together. "It seems like longer than that to me. I'm tired of nothing but meat all the time. What I wouldn't give for a good mess of turnip greens and some corn on the cob!"

"Yeah, the grub's not much," Reb agreed, "but it's been fun." He picked up the long vine rope that Wash had woven for him. It was thicker than he liked, but it was good and strong. "Where'd you learn to weave stuff like this?"

"I don't know." Wash shrugged. "We always made stuff like this where I come from—baskets and things like that."

Jake looked at what Wash was doing. "Do you think that thing will work?"

Wash looked up at him with indignation. "When I make a thing," he said firmly, "it works."

"Well, I don't see how you could ever catch a fish in that, but I sure could use a good plateful of nice, fresh fish."

Wash stood and picked up one end of the affair he had been working on. "It's real easy," he said. He held it up and demonstrated as he talked. "You see, this is the big part of the net—the main part of the trap. Up here—" he pointed "—you got a little opening with a kind of a tunnel, getting smaller as it goes in. What happens is, you put some bait in there. The fish go in this little tunnel and get the bait, but they ain't got sense enough to get out such a small opening. So they just swim around. You pull up the trap, and that's it!" He looked at Jake and Reb scornfully. "I thought everybody knew how to make a fish trap."

"Well, not everybody can do that, and not everybody can lasso like I can." Reb grinned. "Let's go try the thing."

The three boys passed Chief Clag, sitting with his back against a tree. "Chief," Wash said, "I'm going to show you how to catch a fish."

Clag looked up and smiled. "You always show something."

But he looked at the mass of vines curiously. He had shown interest in the projects of the young people. Most of them he approved of since they made life easier. Now he looked at the object that the small black boy held and shook his head. "Fish good. Hard to catch."

As a matter of fact, the tribe had almost no method for catching fish although the river was full of them. The Sleepers had no more wire for hooks, and Wash had come up with the idea of a fish trap.

Clag got to his feet and wandered down to the stream with the boys. As they walked, he examined the braided vine rope in Reb's hands. "What that?"

"I'll show you." He made a loop with the vine rope and said, "Jake, make a run for it."

Jake grinned and took off running. When he was ten feet away, Reb expertly tossed the loop. It sailed through the air and fell over Jake. He pulled it tight, bringing up the boy to a dead halt. "That's what it's for," he said.

Clag looked amused but said, "Why you want catch boy?"

"I don't know." Reb shrugged. "We used to catch cows." Then a thought came to him, and he said, "I bet I could catch one of those wild deer—or maybe even a goat."

The idea interested Clag, and Reb talked about the possibilities until they got to the river. There Reb and the chief sat down to watch as Wash put a bit of meat inside the trap. He tied a long, strong vine rope to the end of the trap and said, "I've found us a good deep spot. There's bound to be fish down there."

He put a rock in the bottom of the trap and tossed it into the water, where it sank at once. Then he tied the free end of the vine rope to a branch. "Pretty soon we'll catch us a fish, I bet."

While they waited, Reb was interested in Clag's weapon—the stone ax. It was the only kind of weapon The People had. "You know, Chief. I've been thinking about a better kind of weapon for you."

"Better than ax?"

"Well, in some ways. I'm surprised nobody's thought of it. It's called a spear." He explained how a spear works, and Clag at once saw the advantage of it.

"We get Beno make stone for end." He nodded, and a light of unexpected humor gleamed in his face. He was a very intelligent man, Reb had found, although tremendously superstitious. "Better stand off far and kill tiger than get close with ax. Get hurt that way."

"You mean to tell me you've killed a tiger with that ax of yours!" Jake exclaimed.

Clag pulled aside his fur garment, and they saw a wicked, ragged scar down his side. "Big tiger. Almost kill me, but I get him."

"Wow," said Wash almost reverently. "Think of that —a tiger with a stone ax."

They sat beside the stream talking until, about an hour later, Wash said, "I think I'll see if we've got anything." He untied the vine and started pulling in the fish trap. "It's heavy!" he yelled. "And I feel it move. Come and give me a hand."

Clag leaped to help and began to pull on the vine. His powerful muscles rolled, and soon the trap was up. Inside were the silver bodies of fish thrashing wildly, and Clag let out a yell. "Fish!" he screamed. He pulled the basket to shore and stood staring at it. He looked at Wash as if the boy were a magician. "How you know this?"

"Oh, it's something we did in our country, Chief. I bet they're good to eat."

"I see." Clag reached into the trap and pulled out a long fish. To Reb's horror he opened his mouth and tore off a section of the fish's body with his teeth. He chomped hard, bones and all, then looked at the boys. "Good!"

Reb said hastily, "Hey, Chief! I bet I can show you a better way to eat fish."

"How?"

That led to their making their way back up to the cave where Jake managed to teach The People how to cook the fish—in a way. They tried to fry some, but there was no grease, so it was easy to burn them.

"I guess they'd call these 'blackened fish,'" Josh said. "They used to eat 'em a lot like that in Louisiana."

Dave was picking at his fish carefully. "I wish we had some hushpuppies to go with them."

"What hushpuppy?" Eena asked curiously.

"Oh, just another kind of bread. I'll show you sometime," Dave answered quickly.

After the meal, the Sleepers sat around the fire, and Clag asked questions about where they lived.

When he finally grew quiet, Dave said, "Chief, tell us something about Greska, the god you serve."

But Clag glanced over at Grak, the medicine man, seated against the cave wall, staring, scowling. "*You* tell," he said.

Grak grunted. "Greska strong!" He went ahead to tell how the god Greska could do almost anything.

When he finished, Dave said, "We serve Goél. He is strong, but he is merciful." He tried to explain something about mercy and truth and gentleness.

Grak snorted. "Bah! Your god weak! Our god strong!"

"I guess I'm not very good at explaining things," Dave said afterward. "I wish Goél were here."

"I do too," said Abbie. "I don't see how we're ever going to do these people any good. They don't have any idea at all about treating other people right."

"Well, they've come up a rough way. It's kill or be killed around here. We'll just do the best we can."

The next day Josh and the other Sleepers got a surprise. They were down at the river fishing with the fish trap when Jake said, "I wonder where Reb is? He went off a couple of hours ago."

"I hope he's careful. He might run into a T-rex or something else out there," Sarah muttered. "Those animals give me the willies."

"Reb can take care of himself," Josh said. "He proved that back at Camelot, didn't he?" He grinned. "I'll never forget him jousting, knocking those knights off into the dirt. He's some guy."

Sarah was sitting on the grass beside him. She leaned over until her shoulder touched his. "Yes, he is. But he's not Josh Adams," she whispered.

Josh blushed. "Aw, Sarah—!" And then he lifted his head. "What's that?"

"Sounds like Reb," Wash answered. "He's yelling. Maybe something's wrong!"

Josh and the other Sleepers jumped up and ran toward the woods.

Just then, out from the trees came a sight Josh would never forget. There was Bob Lee Jackson, his light blue eyes fairly blazing, his cowboy hat pulled firmly over his head—riding a dinosaur!

"Reb!" Dave shouted. "What in the world—"

But Reb was yelling at the top of his lungs. It was, Josh knew, the old Rebel yell, keen and piercing. And suddenly Reb jerked off his hat and began beating the creature he was riding with it as if he were riding a bucking bronco!

Jake stared at the beast and said, "That's a Stegosaurus. At least it's a lot like one."

The dinosaur was not full-grown. When it was, it would be twenty feet high at the shoulder. Now it ambled along on four legs, its long head moving from side to side. Reb had fashioned a bridle of braided vines and put it in its mouth so that he could turn the creature's head one direction or another. The animal had a long tail with some wicked looking spikes on the end of it.

"Watch out for the tail," Reb yelled. "That ain't no fun to fool with." He was straddling the upright plates that seemed to protect the creature and was obviously having the time of his life. He yanked back on the harness then, and the creature stopped.

Reb slipped off, moved quickly to the dinosaur's head, and put his arm around the long neck. The reptile seemed docile enough, and Reb grinned at his friends, his face alive with excitement. "Ain't he a caution now?"

"How'd you get him, Reb?" Dave demanded.

"Well, there was a whole herd of these things down the way. This little fellow wandered off. I had my rope with me, so I just dropped the noose over him. He didn't fight at all. Matter of fact, I think he likes me." He pulled down a tree branch and held out the tender leaves to the animal. "I call him 'Pretty Boy.' He's not a bronco, but he's the closest thing to it."

"When he grows up, you won't be able to handle him," Josh said.

"I know, but maybe we can have some fun till then."

"Hey! You know what?" Wash said. "I bet we could rig up a plow." He looked at the dinosaur's huge legs. "And I bet he could pull one."

"Pull a plow? This ain't no mule. Are you, Pretty Boy?" Reb stroked the smooth nose, and the animal turned his head toward him, seeming to recognize his voice.

And then the Sleepers were suddenly surrounded. When they heard Reb's scream, The People must have hidden in the recesses of the big cave. Now they came down, and the men gathered around the dinosaur.

It was Lom who said, "Good, we eat tonight."

But Reb turned and planted his feet. "Not on your life, Lom. I caught Pretty Boy. He's mine."

Lom glared. "We eat!"

An argument took place, and it looked as though the two would fight until Clag said, "No, he catch. It his."

Lom glared again at Reb and stalked off angrily.

"Looks like Lom's gonna be hard to get along with," Reb said with regret. "And that's too bad. He's a nice fellow. He's just one of those that has to prove how tough they are every morning."

At mid-morning, after the hunters had gone out to hunt game, Dave decided to try to catch more fish. The other boys had gone with the hunters, so he was alone. As he picked up the trap and started for the river, Eena said, "I go with you."

"Sure, come along."

But Sarah drew Dave off to one side. "Dave, don't you think you're spending too much time with that girl? In the first place, you're going to make Lom more angry. In the second place . . . well . . . it's just not smart for you to be seeing so much of her."

"What's wrong with that?"

Sarah's face grew thoughtful. "These people are simple, Dave. You know that. Eena's almost old enough to take a mate. That's what she's thinking of, and you know that can't be you. It may be Lom. But what if she falls in love with you?"

Dave shook his head. "Oh, that's crazy, Sarah. You're just too romantic! I'm just going fishing, and she's going with me. That's all there is to it."

"Dave, you're the leader," Sarah said evenly, her face very serious. "It's up to you to show wisdom and be careful about how things *look*. Do you think it's wise to give that girl encouragement?"

But Dave was angered by her words. "You take care of your business, Sarah. I'll take care of mine." He turned and said, "Come on, Eena."

As the two of them walked off toward the river, Eena asked, "Why you yell at Sarah?"

"Oh, she just has funny ideas." Dave grinned. "Women are like that."

"Like what?"

"Why, they're—they're just funny, that's all. With a guy I always know where I am. But girls, they've got romantic ideas."

"What 'romantic'?"

Dave set out on a long-winded explanation.

When he had finally finished explaining romance and courtship, Eena seemed intrigued. "Where you come from, males bring presents to females?"

"Sure. Flowers and candy and stuff."

"What 'candy,' and what 'stuff'?"

Dave laughed. "Well, that'll take some explaining. Let's get to fishing."

When they got to the river they found that the heavy rains of the night before had turned the placid stream into a swift-flowing torrent. White water was everywhere.

"I doubt if we'll catch anything," Dave said. "The river's too high. But we'll try."

He baited the net, threw it into the water, and then sat back to wait. The sun was warm, and he dozed off.

He woke up hearing screams. He sprang to his feet and saw that Eena—had she gone to look at the fish trap?—had fallen into the river.

"Eena!" he yelled.

She was being carried off by the swift water, and it was obvious she couldn't swim.

Dave kicked off his shoes and took a running dive. The raging water grabbed him, but he was a strong swimmer. He reached Eena, and she clutched at him and pulled him under. He broke her hold, turned her around, kicked to the surface. Holding her head high, he said, "Don't fight me, Eena. I've got you!"

He dragged her to shore, and the two sat on the riverbank, gasping. She was spitting and coughing but was finally able to say, "I die in river, if you no pull out."

"Well, I was a lifeguard at a summer camp . . ."

Eena put her hand on his. There were few words in the language of the tribe to express gratitude, but apparently she had heard the Sleepers from time to time say something when they received a favor. Now she leaned toward him and said, "Thank you."

Eena's face was close to his. She was a very attractive girl. Dave blushed and said, "Oh, that's all right, Eena. I'm glad I was around. You'll have to be more careful though. Stay away from the river when it's high like that."

73

"You good, Dave."

Dave was flattered by her attentions, but he knew better than to get in deeper. Jumping up, he pulled her to her feet. "Well, no fish today. Let's go back."

When they returned to camp, Dave said nothing of the incident, but Eena began telling everybody how he had pulled her out of the river and saved her life.

Reb, who had been riding around on Pretty Boy, teaching him a trick or two, grinned and said, "You're just a hero, ain't you, Dave? Trust you to find a pretty girl and save her life. Never seen you to fail."

Lom, of course, heard the story.

That night, as Dave was speaking to Eena, the young warrior confronted him. "You stay away from Eena." Without warning he doubled up his fist and hit Dave squarely on the jaw. Dave fell flat on his back. Lom stood glowering over him and said, "You fight for her."

Dave saw that the chief was watching. His eyes swept around, and he saw that his friends too were waiting to see what he would do. They knew him to have a hot temper, and now they expected him to jump up and fight Lom.

Instead, he got up slowly and shook his head. "No, we didn't come to fight you, Lom," he said seriously. "We came because Goél wants you to have a better life."

At that the witch doctor shouted, "No! Last night I have dream." He began going into what seemed to be a fit. His shoulders shook, and his face twisted. "In darkness, someone come. Strong. Mighty. He say we no follow Goél. He say Goél weak. We no listen to strangers. We follow Dark Lord."

At the words "Dark Lord," all the Sleepers stiffened.

Dave heard Josh murmur to Sarah. "The Dark Lord! Somehow he's here—even in this place!"

74

"I'm afraid, Josh," Sarah said. "We know what he can do. He can lead these people into disaster."

The wrinkled witch doctor screamed and worked himself into a frenzy. At last he stopped before the chief and said, "We no follow Goél—we follow Greska."

"Don't listen to him, Chief," Dave said desperately. "The Dark Lord—he's out there in our world too, and he always brings death and terror. But the way of Goél brings peace and light."

"Show us Goél," Clag demanded.

"Well," Dave said lamely, "we can't do that. But he's always nearby, and he's good." But he saw the chief's eyes were on the witch doctor, and he knew that he had failed.

8
Sarah's Admirer

Dave was working with Beno on a secret project. He did not tell any of the Sleepers what they were doing, but every day he managed to get to the small cave Beno used for a workshop.

Today, as usual, Beno beamed up at him. "What you make today?"

Dave thought for a moment, then said, "You and I are going to make something that will turn the world upside down. This world, anyway."

Beno stared at him. "We stand on head?"

Dave laughed. "No, no. I have an idea, but I'll need your help."

Beno nodded eagerly. "Yes, Beno help. You show."

Dave pulled a pencil and a small piece of paper from his pocket and began sketching.

Beno seemed fascinated. He watched carefully, and, when Dave had finished, he looked at the paper. "You want Beno make this?"

"Yes, exactly that size. Can you do it?"

Beno shrugged. "I make. Easy." He looked again at the sketch. "What it for?"

"It's called an arrowhead. Don't tell anybody. I want it to be a surprise, but I'll show you how it works. You put this on one end of a straight, round stick. Then you put feathers on the other end. It's called an arrow."

"How long stick?"

Dave spread his hands to show him.

"Not big enough for spear. Ax head too little."

"It's not an ax head—it's an arrow. Look, what we'll do is—I'll go find the right kind of wood and cut a piece of it —whittle it down. Then we'll tie it like this." He sketched carefully. "When you put the back of the arrow on this piece of vine and pull it back and let go, it goes through the air. It flies. You can be far away from something and kill it without getting close." He took some time to explain the principle, and then Beno brightened. "That be good! You make bow. I make arrowhead."

Dave clapped him on the shoulder. "Make as many as you can while I do the rest of it."

He left Beno's work cave and spent the rest of the morning searching for wood that would do for a bow. He had been interested in archery back in Oldworld. He had even made a bow or two. *I'll make do,* he said to himself. *This invention will turn this whole tribe around!*

He gathered enough wood to make several shafts and wondered what he would use for feathers. "We'll just have to trap some birds. There's plenty of them around." He glanced up even then and saw the leathery form of a pterodactyl flapping lazily across the sky. "No feathers on that thing!" He grinned. "Looks like maybe he'd be good to make a catcher's mitt."

He returned to the big cave, piled the sticks in the little corner reserved for himself, and covered them with his blanket. Everyone else was out, so he grew curious and went to find them.

He heard shouting coming from far off and followed the sound until he found Reb riding Pretty Boy, as usual. The sight always entertained the tribespeople and amused the seven Sleepers as well.

Reb drew Pretty Boy to a halt, pulled his Stetson off, and waved it. "Hey, Dave! You want to ride?"

"I guess not," Dave called back with a smile. "I had a hard enough time staying on a horse and—"

Just then a woman screamed.

Dave looked up to see a terrible sight. A ferocious-looking dinosaur was emerging from the trees!

He had always thought dinosaurs were huge, ponderous beasts. This one seemed not much more than six feet tall, but it had frightful-looking spurs on the back of its feet that could rip open the toughest hide. It also had fierce, sharp teeth.

The men grabbed their clubs and positioned themselves, Clag at the point and Lom beside him. The women and children ran screaming up the path toward the cave.

Dave wanted to join them but was ashamed to. He saw that Josh had picked up a club from somewhere and was advancing to stand beside Lom.

I can't let Josh do it without me! Not seeing a club, he seized a rock and took his place in the line. Clag looked over at him and nodded, but his face was serious. Dave knew the chief had had experience with these swift beasts before.

The dinosaur plowed into the line, bowling over Clag and narrowly missing him with one of its vicious spurs. Lom swung his ax mightily and caught the brute on the side of the neck.

The blow stopped the creature for a moment, but then the snakelike head whirled around toward Lom. It was only because several members of the tribe were hacking at the reptile that Lom did not receive the terrible claws in his chest.

The battle raged on. Several men were down with gaping wounds. Others continued wielding their axes. Reb picked up a stout pole and brought it down with both hands over the animal's back.

But at last the collective assault won out, and Clag struck the beast a final blow on the head. With a groan the dinosaur slowly collapsed.

Dave looked around at the wounded men. "It's a good thing there weren't *two* dinosaurs," he said.

Clag gave a nod of agreement.

Lom was breathing hard. All he said was, "We eat tonight."

For the next two hours the men were busy hauling the dinosaur carcass back to the cave, looking over their shoulders constantly for a mate. As usual, they butchered the creature immediately and made preparations for a feast.

Several men were cut up badly, and Sarah cleansed many wounds. One of those she treated was the hunter Raddy—the one who followed her around and stared at her curiously.

The fire burned high in the cave that night. The smell of burned meat was in the air. Dave was sitting close to his blanket, thinking how to best make the bow and the arrows, when Raddy walked over to him.

Raddy was a short, squat individual with quick, dark eyes and a mass of black hair that fell continually over those eyes. "You, Chief, I talk you."

Dave blinked in surprise. Chief? The idea seemed strange, and yet had not Goél put him in charge? He said, "What is it, Raddy?"

Raddy grinned. He was missing several teeth, which gave him a rather comical appearance. He nodded toward Sarah and said, "Me have her."

"What do you mean, you 'have her'?"

"Raddy no have mate. He take her."

Reb covered a broad grin with his hand and shook with silent laughter.

Dave noticed but knew this was no laughing matter. "Raddy, we don't do things like that where we come from." He tried to explain that it was impossible for Sarah to become his mate.

But Raddy was determined. "Raddy good hunter. Make good mate," he insisted.

Dave felt the eyes of the chief on him. "Clag, you understand that as a chief I can do some things but not other things."

"Give him girl," Clag said. "He good man."

Dave cleared his throat but shook his head. "No, I'm sorry, but we can't do that."

Raddy continued to argue but finally grew sullen and walked away, kicking at a rock as he went. He sat down across the cave, his back against the wall, and glowered at Dave.

"You're not making many friends, are you, Dave?" Jake said. "What if he insists on it?"

"Oh, don't be ridiculous, Jake!" Sarah said quickly. "It's just silly."

"Not to him it isn't." Jake shrugged. "I guess he's paid you a pretty high compliment, Sarah."

"We've got to be careful," Josh said. "Can't think of any way to get in a bigger mess than to get mixed up with a thing like this. You'll have to make it clear to him, Dave."

Dave was edgy and snapped back. "I suppose you could do better!"

Josh put up his hands. "I wasn't criticizing, but you can see how serious it is."

But Dave grew withdrawn and moody.

The next morning, he took his knife and his wood and went out to a place he thought was far enough away to work on his bow and arrows.

He had worked for quite a while when suddenly a noise to his right startled him. He jumped up, gripping the knife. "Who's that?"

"Me—Eena." She stepped from behind a tree and sat

down beside him. She looked at his work. "What you make?"

"Oh, just something I think might help the tribe."

That obviously satisfied her. Then she said, "Why you no give Sarah to Raddy? He good hunter."

"Well, in our country," Dave said slowly, "we don't give people away. What happens is, a young man sees a young woman, and if he likes her—and she likes him— they begin to go places together."

"Go what places?"

Dave thought of the difficulty of explaining a McDonald's or a movie or a baseball game. "Oh, just to look at pretty things like the trees and the river and—just to be together. After a while, if he likes her enough, he asks her to be his mate. And if she likes him, she says yes."

"And then what?"

"Why, then they become mates. That's not your way, I know, but that's the way Sarah's used to. It wouldn't be right to her to do it any other way."

Dave picked up the knife and began to work on the bow again. It was pleasant sitting there in the sun, and Eena was good company. For two hours he worked, and she questioned him until he had told her what little he knew about courtship.

"Here," she said, "the father give woman to man that he like."

"What if *she* doesn't like him?"

That possibility seemed not to have occurred to her. She shrugged. After a long silence she said, "I like better your way."

Dave finally had the bow in good shape. "I've got to find some real strong vines, very strong and very small. Can you show me some, Eena?"

"Yes, come."

Together they collected vines that could be woven to make a bowstring. Then Dave gathered up his things, wrapped them in the piece of cloth he had brought for that purpose, and they headed back toward the cave.

Josh met them, wearing a strange expression. "You've been gone a long time."

Dave realized that what he had done didn't look good, but he would not admit he was wrong. "I'm doing something very important," he said. "I needed Eena to help me."

Josh looked at him even more severely. "What are you making? What's going on?"

Dave hesitated, then said, "I'm making a bow and arrows. See!" He unfolded the cloth and showed Josh the six-foot-long bow that was practically finished and the shafts for the arrows. "All I need is the arrowheads, and Beno's making those. And we'll need some feathers. Then we'll have something to show the tribe."

Josh hesitated. "I don't know, Dave. It's not always a good idea to rush people. Letting them find their own way sometimes may be best."

"What do you mean? You didn't object to showing them how to make bread."

"I know, but this could change the whole balance of things in this world. Can you imagine what would happen if one tribe had bows and arrows and the other had only clubs?"

"We're just going to use these to *hunt*."

Josh gave him an impatient glance. "How can you guarantee that? You know better, Dave. Just like in Old-world when countries began arming up with nuclear weapons. Everybody knew that sooner or later somebody would use them."

Dave laughed unpleasantly. "Arrows and nuclear weapons—they're not the same at all."

Josh must have known he was wasting his breath. "Maybe having bows and arrows could be a good thing—but it isn't good for you to be running around through the woods with Eena all day long, and you know that."

If Dave had felt a little less guilty, he might have been more ready to accept Josh's criticism. Now, though, since he knew he was wrong, he said, "Just keep your mouth shut, Josh. I'm the leader on this trek. I followed you when you were the leader. So let's have no more criticizing. I know what I'm doing." He turned around and walked off.

Eena followed him.

Josh looked up at the sky in despair. "I wish you were here, Goél. I don't think things are going too well."

9
Dave's Scheme Backfires

Lom led the hunters back to the big cave and was met by practically the whole village. When they saw the large, deerlike creature the men carried, a cry of joy went up. "We eat tonight!"

As the men cut up the game and the fire was building, Lom walked over to Eena. He held up his club and shook it. His dark eyes gleamed. He was clearly filled with pride over the exploit.

He began to tell her about how he had killed the deer, and soon most of the Sleepers themselves were gathered around with the tribespeople, listening. Lom was a good storyteller and had the group fascinated with his tale.

"He doesn't mind bragging, does he?" Dave murmured to Abbie.

"I guess it's a big thing. After all, success in hunting's the biggest thing in a young man's life in this culture. It's life or death to them."

"I guess so, but it looks like he could just do it and not brag about it." Dave was scowling, and Abbie looked at him thoughtfully but said nothing more.

When the fire blazed high, the whole tribe gathered inside the cavern, and once again the Sleepers observed a feast of the cave people. The women, as usual, impaled small portions of meat on sticks, roasted them over the fire, then handed them out to the men.

Reb pulled his off the stick and juggled it to keep from burning his fingers. Carefully he bit into it but then cried,

"Ouch! Burned my tongue off. Sure wish I had a good bit of possum to go with this."

"Possum!" Jake said. "How could you eat one of those things? They look like a big rat! I'll bet they're greasy too."

"Well," Reb said thoughtfully, "they do slide down pretty good. But I'd sure like to have some. I miss the stuff we used to have—like a Quarter Pounder at McDonald's maybe."

"Now you're talking!" Jake nodded enthusiastically. "And what wouldn't I give for a good milkshake from TCBY."

The two sat there naming different favorite foods until Josh said, "I wish you two would shut up. You're making me hungry."

"Doesn't do any good to talk about that anyway," Dave grumbled. He picked at his meat. "We just have to make the best of what we've got."

At that point, as usual, there was a time of storytelling. And this evening Lom was the hero of the hunt. He got up and repeated his story, acting it out this time. His strong young body, muscular and lithe, glistened in the firelight as he reenacted the chase.

Sarah noticed that Lom kept his eyes fixed on Eena, and she leaned over to whisper to Josh. "He's a fine-looking fellow. He and Eena may be together one of these days."

"Well, I feel sorry for Beno," Josh answered. "Look at him."

Sarah looked over at the lame young man, his back against the wall. He sat away from the fire, alone. "He's a fine-looking guy too. Looks more like a poet than a hunter, though. And he looks lonesome. I think I'll go over and sit by him."

When she sat down beside Beno, he looked at her with surprise. "That was a good story, Beno," she said. "But he couldn't have killed that thing without your ax head, could he now?"

A warm light came into Beno's brown eyes. But then he looked over sadly at the muscular warrior. "I wish I could hunt," he said simply.

Sarah had no answer, but she stayed with Beno, trying to cheer up the young man.

Meantime Dave grew more and more gloomy. Finally, when Lom sat down, he said to Josh, "I'm going to show them what I've got. It's time this bunch got to be a little bit more scientific."

"The bow and arrows? I wouldn't do that if I were you. It could lead to trouble."

Dave glared. "Oh, you're just a worrywart, Josh! It'll revolutionize this tribe. You're just old-fashioned." Then he unwrapped his weapon.

Holding up the bow and one arrow, he cried out, "Chief, I have a gift for your people!"

His voice carried throughout the cave, and Clag and all his people looked at him with surprise. Not one of the visitors had ever before taken part in any of the ceremonies at a feast.

"What this?" Clag demanded.

"This is a weapon!" Dave lifted up the bow in one hand and the single arrow in the other. "With this you can kill animals from far away."

At once Clag showed interest. He stepped forward and peered closely at the bow, but then shook his head. "Too weak. It break."

Dave laughed. "No. You don't *hit* the animal with it." He mimicked inflicting a blow as with a club. "I'll show you tomorrow. We go on a hunt. I'll kill an animal from as far away as from here to the side of the cave."

A murmur went up from the hunters, and there was doubt in every face. On Lom's face was disgust. "Big talk," he said.

Dave glared. "You'll see. Tomorrow you'll see." Then he made the mistake of smiling at Eena and saying, "Princess Eena, tomorrow I'll bring you a fine meal."

She smiled up at him, her face glowing in the firelight.

Josh glanced at Lom and whispered to Sarah, "That's two mistakes. He's making Lom jealous, and that can be downright deadly in this place. Second, I'm not at all sure about teaching them that kind of weaponry. I wish he wouldn't do it, but he's stubborn."

"It seems he's gotten that way," Sarah agreed. "He's really a sweet boy, but he's got to do this, I think, to prove himself." She smiled at Josh. "He's got a very good leader to beat, Josh."

Josh blushed. "This isn't a popularity contest. I just wish he'd let this thing alone."

The next morning the hunters left at dawn.

Dave said, "Chief, I don't know how to find game, but if you'll find me something, I'll show you how to bring it down without even touching it."

He had made a leather quiver, and the four arrows he and Beno had fashioned were in it. He carried the six-foot bow, unstrung, and indeed it looked feeble enough.

Clag led the party. They traveled steadily for three hours, and by the time they got to a place that satisfied the chief, Dave was almost winded. *I wish,* he thought, *I could run as far as these guys do. They'd sure make good marathon runners back home.*

The chief raised his arm and pointed toward a thicket, then to the ground. "See. Game inside bush!" He looked at the flimsy bow in Dave's hand and said, "We drive. You kill."

Dave caught his meaning. Clag sent four hunters out wide, and Dave knew whatever was in the thicket would be driven toward him soon.

Quickly he attached the vine string to the bow. Then, reaching back, he pulled out an arrow, almost three feet long. He put the notch on the string, allowed it to fall upon the top of his fist, and gave a tentative pull. He had made the bow much thicker than normal, knowing that whatever he shot at would be tough.

He turned sideways, pulled it back to full draw, his right hand underneath his right ear, and sighted down the arrow. "Ought to do it," he said, "if they don't drive a t-rex out of there."

He carefully eased off on the string and began to advance toward the thicket. He heard Clag cautioning the others to stay back, and he heard Lom's snort of disbelief. Cautiously Dave moved forward.

Now the hunters Clag had sent out were yelling and beating the bushes.

When Dave was thirty feet from the thicket, he stopped and planted his feet. "Ought to be about right," he said rather nervously. "I just hope they don't drive anything too mean out of there."

Then he heard a thrashing. The bushes moved, and an animal charged through the thicket. Dave raised the bow and held it steady. It seemed not to be a large animal —at least not one as dangerous as a t-Rex—but at first he couldn't see what it was for the shrubs. And then it exploded into the clear. A razorback pig! *The biggest one I ever saw!*

The boar was fully four feet tall at the shoulder. It had a pair of red, piggish eyes and huge, sharp tusks like knives going up from each side of its snout. It was heavy in the shoulders and narrow in the flanks—and it spotted Dave at once. With a wild, brutish snort, the pig threw itself forward.

Dave almost panicked. *If I miss, he'll rip me open with those tusks! I can't miss!*

As the boar headed straight for him, Dave took a deep breath and pulled the bow back to his ear. He strained with the effort. *Got to wait!* he thought. *I'll only get one chance.*

Dave let the pig take two more steps—then, sighting down the arrow, he breathed a quick cry for help to Goél and released the string.

Twang!

He had no chance to flee, and his heart was in his throat. Then he saw the arrow strike the boar squarely in the chest. The enraged pig still almost got to him before it weakened. Dave leaped aside, and the boar made one sweep with its jaws, catching him on the leg. Dave's calf felt as if it had been touched with a hot iron, and he rolled to the ground thinking, *He's got me!*

But the boar gave a series of snorts, then collapsed. Its feet kicked wildly, and then they fell still.

A wild yell came from the hunters.

Then Dave felt strong hands pulling him to his feet. Clag was holding him by the shoulders, his eyes wild with excitement. "You great hunter!" he exclaimed. He picked up the bow and held it as if it were magic. His eyes were reverent. "This good!"

Dave breathed a sigh of relief.

He noticed, however, that Lom hung back. Lom did not join the crowd of eager hunters that came to admire the bow and the dead pig. Dave thought, *Wait till I tell the story tonight. Then we'll see.*

Back at the cave the Sleepers were glad to see Dave. But Sarah saw his bloody leg at once. "Your leg! You've been hurt!"

"Oh, that's nothing." Dave shrugged. "Just a scratch."

"No, I'd better put some antiseptic on it. You're not as tough as these folks."

She dressed his leg, and the others gathered around as Dave told his story. His eyes were alive with excitement. "You should have seen Clag's face. I'll tell you, he was amazed!"

Later that night, after the boar had been roasted and eaten, every stomach was full, and there was a good air about the crowd, Clag said, "Today you tell."

Dave got up, looked over at Lom, then smiled. He began to tell the story of the hunt and threw himself into it. The warriors accompanied him with yells when he told how the boar had gone down.

As soon as he finished, he sat down beside Reb, who looked at him with an odd light in his eye.

"I thought you said yesterday that Lom was bragging too much. You didn't sound like any shrinking violet to me."

Dave shifted uncomfortably. He knew he had been boastful—and wished he hadn't been quite so much like the young hunter. But it was too late now.

Then the chief came over. Dave stood, and Clag began to make a long-winded speech about how brave this young man was and how wonderful things were going to be. "This bow, you call it. You make more?"

"Oh, yes." Dave did have one gracious moment. He went over and put his hand on Beno's shoulder. "It wouldn't have been possible without Beno, Chief. Arrows must have arrowheads." He patted Beno benevolently. "This is the man that makes it all work."

As Dave said this, he happened to glance at Eena. He saw her eyes go to the young craftsman. He saw her thoughtful look.

But Clag was going on with his speech. "You and Beno make many bow. Many arrow." He held up one.

"Yes, we can do that."

Then Clag said, "Good. When we have many bow and arrow, we go kill Mord's men. Take their women!"

A wild yell went up from the hunters, and Dave looked aghast.

Josh came over. "I think we're in trouble, Dave. We've got a war on our hands now. I don't think this is exactly what Goél sent us here to do!"

10
The Captive

It's a good thing Beno can't turn out arrowheads like a factory," Josh said to Sarah. They were walking along the river.

"You mean a war is going to start as soon as Clag gets enough bows and arrows to arm the tribe?" She looked out over the water thoughtfully, watching a huge log float along as she spoke.

"That's right. We've got to do something, Sarah! We can't let the tribe kill other people with those arrows!"

"But what can we do? Clag won't listen to any talk of peace. We've already tried that."

For several days they had met with the chief, who had listened impatiently as various members of the Sleepers tried to tell him that it would be better not to kill Mord's tribe.

"We no kill them, they kill us!" he argued.

Dave had been quiet ever since his scheme backfired. He suggested once to Beno that perhaps he shouldn't make more arrowheads. But Clag knew that Beno was able to make them, and that settled it.

Reb had been engaged in the pursuits he enjoyed, making lariats out of vines and teaching some of the tribesmen to lasso things. He had little success however, for they were clumsy.

"Good night!" he said. "Back where I come from, even the babies in the cradle know how to rope."

He made a loop and began to spin it. It grew larger and larger. He stepped inside it like a circus performer, a grin on his face. "Now, that's the way you're supposed to make it work." Then he suddenly made the loop fly up and over toward Grak, the witch doctor, who was standing a few feet away. The loop fell across his shoulders, and Reb yanked it tight.

Grak let out a wild yell and tried to run, but he was held fast.

The watching hunters immediately fell silent, but Reb laughed. He walked over and released the medicine man. "Just a little fun," he said.

But Grak's small black eyes glittered. His lips worked, and he uttered a string of meaningless syllables.

At once the hunters broke and ran as if a dinosaur had suddenly appeared.

"Well, what got into them?" Reb scratched his head.

"I think," Jake said, "the old man just put a curse on you."

"A curse? I don't believe in that stuff!" Reb shrugged carelessly.

"I don't either," Jake said, "but *they* do. Watch out for that old buzzard. He looked like he'd like to slip a knife in your ribs."

Later that afternoon Reb went to the chief. "Jake and I are going out on our own hunt. Gonna bring something back alive."

Clag was interested in any kind of hunt and wanted to go along. He nodded to Lom and four other men, indicating that they should join the hunting party.

An hour later, Jake was puffing for breath. "I don't like this. Anything could happen out here. It's like living in a zoo, only inside the cages. All we need is one saber-toothed tiger to end everything!"

Reb gave him a look. "You're the most pessimistic human I ever saw, Jake. Let's look at the good side of it. Maybe we *won't* get et by a tiger. Think about that."

Reb had been scouting out the land and knew what he was looking for. He held up his hand.

The chief's eyes were bright. "What you do?" he demanded.

"There's some kind of ox critter over there. I aim to get him, and then we'll see. You let me have first shot, all right?"

"What is 'shot'?"

Reb shook his head. "I sure wish you'd talk Southern," he said mournfully. "Let me do the hunting this time, all right?"

"What is 'all right'?"

"It means—oh, never mind! Stay here. Send your men out and drive that critter toward me."

Clag looked doubtful. "Big horns. Once many hunters be kill with horns from that kind."

"He won't kill me. You just drive him my way."

The hunters fanned out and, in their accomplished fashion, soon began yelling to drive the game out of the brush.

Jake said, "I hope they don't drive nothing too big out of there. Are you sure this is going to work?"

"Shore it'll work! My mama didn't sponsor no failures. Look out—here it comes!"

Not one but a half-dozen wild oxen came crashing out of the thicket toward them.

Jake let out a yelp and made for a tree. He scrambled up it like a monkey.

The hunters, including the chief, took cover as well.

But Reb held his ground. He had his Stetson pulled down firmly over his forehead, and his light blue eyes gleamed with excitement. As the small herd thundered toward him, Reb spotted what he wanted—two yearlings, big enough for trouble but not monstrous like the full-grown animals.

The four adults charged past. Reb sidestepped neatly and let them go, but he kept his eye on the two younger animals. When they were even with him, he swung the vine rope over his head, and when the larger of the two flashed by, he let fly with his lariat.

The loop spread wide. It opened up in front of the animal's legs.

Reb knew there would be a hard jolt, so when the loop closed, he dug in his heels. If he'd gotten the animal around the neck, he would have been dragged along, but the noose closed on the yearling's front legs. Although it jerked Reb to the ground, the animal fell, uttering a series of piercing snorts.

Reb was pulled along several feet, but he let out a wild, "Yippee, I got him!" and scrambled to his feet.

He ran to the ox, which was struggling to get up, and sat on its head. "You just set there, young feller," he said. "I got plans for you."

Clag and the rest scurried down from the trees and came over, babbling.

"That was pretty good roping," Jake said. "If there was a Madison Square Garden here I guess you'd win first prize at the rodeo."

"Wasn't too bad." The animal was still thrashing about. "Hold him down, you fellers, while I get him ready to take home."

Several of the hunters restrained the young ox, and Reb cut two short pieces of vine and tied its front feet together. "OK, you can let him up now. He ain't going nowhere," he said cheerfully.

The tribe watched the beast struggle to its feet, look around, try to run. It was tripped immediately by the hob-

96

ble. This went on for at least ten falls. Finally the animal was exhausted, and Reb untied its legs.

"I reckon he's ready now." Reb cut off another short piece of his vine rope and fashioned it into a bridle. It went through the animal's mouth and back over its neck. The yearling tugged at it.

"Come along now. You'll get to like us."

The animal was hard to lead. Time and again it would try to run, but Reb would jerk its head back. By the time they'd gotten halfway back to the cave, the ox was following as gentle as a lamb.

At the cave they were met as usual by the women, who started at once clamoring for something to eat.

"Not this time. I'm going to keep him—along with Pretty Boy," he said. "I'm going to show you something about this fellow in a few days," Reb told the chief.

It was actually a week later. The tribe had gotten accustomed to Reb's going out with the ox, which he had named Stonewall. They would go off together and come back a few hours later.

Finally, one morning Reb said, "Y'all come. I got something to show you."

Clag went along, as did Lom and the rest of the Sleepers. Eena and some of the women followed.

Reb led them to an open field. "Now, you watch this. Me and Beno been working on this." He looped a series of vine ropes over Stonewall's head. The ends of the vines were already tied to what appeared to be sticks fastened together. He grasped the stick contraption by two protruding handles and said, "You ain't never seen this, I reckon."

"Why, it's a *plow!*" Josh said in astonishment.

"Yep, that's what it is. Watch this now." Reb steadied the device, and called out, "Hup, Stonewall! Hup!"

97

The animal lumbered forward, pulling the contraption easily. The plow had a stone point—no doubt made by Beno—that turned over the light soil in a nice furrow.

Then Reb cried out, "Gee, Stonewall! Gee!" Obediently the ox made a wide turn and came back. Reb stopped, looking back at his double furrow. "Look at that!" he said proudly. "Ain't everybody can plow a straight line like that. How do you like it, Chief?"

Clag stared. "What it for?"

"Well, I thought you folks might learn to farm a little bit. Your daughter—Eena here—she's got a mighty good idea. What we need to do is plant these seeds, and pretty soon you'll have a garden."

It took a while to explain the concept of garden to Clag, but he appeared interested.

Lom, however, said in disgust, "Only women play in dirt!" He turned around and walked away, his back straight.

"I guess Lom doesn't care for the idea too much," Josh said, "but it's a good idea, Chief." He tried to explain how they could raise gourds and vegetables and roots. "You won't have to go hunting for them. They'll be right here for you."

Afterward, when the Sleepers gathered for one of their meetings, Josh beamed warmly. "That was fine, Reb. Just the sort of thing that'll help these people."

Dave had said little. He had been subdued ever since his idea of the arrows failed. Now he went off by himself, looking sullen.

Abbie followed him. "What's the matter, Dave? Things are working out pretty well—except for the war that might come."

"If you've come to nag me," Dave snapped, "you can go somewhere else. I don't need it."

"Well, all right," Abbie said stiffly. "If you're going to be that way, I'll just let you alone."

Dave was sorry but was too proud to say so. He walked for a long time by the river, filled with apprehension and doubt. When he was coming back, still thinking about his problems, a shout from the cave took him by surprise.

Something's wrong! He dashed up the path and found all the tribe circled around something he couldn't see. Shoving his way through, he burst into the inner circle.

There stood a young man, someone he'd never seen before, a tall young man with reddish hair that was now down in his eyes. He'd been injured, for blood trickled down his scalp, but he stood fearlessly looking around at the hunters, who were yelling and brandishing axes at him.

"Who's that, Chief?"

Clag was smiling broadly—it was one of the few times Dave had ever seen him show such pleasure. "This Ral."

"Where's he from?"

"He from Mord's tribe. He Ral, son of Mord." He walked up to the young man, who faced him unafraid. His arm had been wounded too, for blood dripped from his elbow.

"You come to spy," Clag grunted, and then he raised his ax.

The young man called Ral still showed not a flicker of fear. "No," he said. "I lost."

"You lie." Grak danced into the circle. He wore a necklace of bones, as usual, and his face was painted yellow and blue. He looked hideous. His screams rent the air. "You die! You die! We give you to Greska."

"No, I kill," Clag said.

But Grak threw himself into one of his fits. He fell on the ground and shrieked. Then he got up and, for an old

99

man, moved surprisingly fast. He danced around the chief and the young enemy warrior, screeching, "He belong to Greska."

Then Clag seemed to relent. He reluctantly nodded at the young warrior. "Yes, give to Greska. Take him to stone."

Strong hands seized Ral and dragged him along. Fists struck him many times, but he uttered not a word.

"We've got to stop this!" Dave gasped.

"If you interfere, you'll take on that old witch doctor," Jake said. "He's got these folks convinced. Why, they're just liable to take us instead, if we mess with their religious ceremony."

But Dave and the other Sleepers followed along, their cries drowned out by the howling warriors, who by now had thrown themselves into a frenzy.

Finally they reached a large, flat rock. Four warriors threw Ral down on it, each holding a hand or foot so that he was spread-eagled.

Then the witch doctor grinned and plucked a sharp stone from the pouch at his waist. He stood over the helpless young man. "We give heart to Greska."

"He's going to cut his heart out!" Josh gasped. "We've got to do *something!*"

But even as Grak raised the razor-sharp stone, there was a sharp cry. Suddenly Eena shoved the witch doctor aside. He stumbled and looked at the girl with hatred. "You die too! He Greska's."

"No!" Eena said firmly.

She gazed down at the young man, who turned his eyes to look up at her. "He not Greska's."

At once a tremendous argument broke out. Half the tribe was for killing the stranger to satisfy Greska, but the other half seemed to be against it. Obviously no one liked Grak, though all feared him.

Finally Dave stepped forward. "Chief, let him live. Keep him as a prisoner. There's a better way than this. It won't do any good to kill him."

Clag actually was caught in the middle. Half of his warriors were for killing the young man, the other half opposed. He seemed glad for any interruption. "Good. We not kill—" he looked at the medicine man "—not yet."

Grak drew his lips together tightly. "Greska angry. Whole tribe suffer."

But when the young man was pulled to his feet, he appeared to be the most surprised one in the crowd. "No kill?" he asked. He looked at Eena strangely. "Why you not let him kill?"

Eena had to look up to face the young man, who was very tall. "I—" She broke off, shook her head, turned around, and walked away to stand beside her father.

"You stay here!" the chief ordered Ral. "No run away, or we kill."

The tall young man looked around at the fierce warriors, his deadly enemies. He nodded slowly. "Yes, I stay."

11
The Raid

Mord's band lived not far from Clag's tribe. This group also dwelled in caves, although smaller ones. Their leader was a strong warrior. He ruled his men with an iron hand as did all leaders in that country. Only by the power of his arm was he ruler, and to show weakness was to invite being dethroned.

Mord was sitting underneath a large, fernlike tree when one of his warriors came running in, out of breath, his eyes wide. "Mord," he gasped, "your son. They have him."

Mord knew that his son Ral had gone hunting with this man. He got to his feet quickly. He lived in a violent world and expected bad news. "Where is he, Roni?" he demanded.

"We went far—close to Clag's country. We chase game very far."

"What of Ral?"

Roni was a smallish man, fleet of foot. He had little, close-set black eyes. "Clag's men catch him."

A fleeting emotion swept over the face of the gigantic warrior chief. He had had three sons, but two of them had died young. Now his tall, blue-eyed son with the same reddish hair he himself had was the pride of his heart. He glared at Roni without a word, then asked, "They kill?"

"No," Roni said. "They take away."

A look of hope came into Mord's face. He was not only a powerful man but was by far the most quick-witted of the entire tribe. "Come. We get every warrior."

Roni stared at his chief. "We go fight Clag?"
"Yes! We go get Ral."

Eena was fascinated by the captive, Ral. She affected to pay no attention to him for a time, yet when the others ate and he was offered nothing, she picked up a piece of charred meat and strolled toward him. He was tied by the ankle to a tree and guarded by Raddy, who sat holding his ax, watching every move the young man made.

"Here!" Eena said loftily. She tossed the meat at the young man. It fell on the stony ground, and he ignored it. His attitude angered her. "You no eat?"

Ral turned his eyes toward her. His auburn hair had a slight curl, and it hung down his back, bound by a single piece of leather. He was large, like his father, and his body was sleek with powerful muscles. Still ignoring the meat, he stared at her.

Eena was provoked. "You no eat, you starve."

Ral looked at the meat, then back at her. "You kill anyway." And then he seemed curious again. "Why you no let witch doctor kill? Me your enemy."

Eena had no answer. She was the child of a blood-thirsty race and had seen men die before. She herself did not understand why she had stopped Grak from ripping the young man's heart from his chest. Something about her act troubled her. It was as if doing a kindness was something she did not comprehend. She turned to go, then wheeled to face him. "You Ral, son of Mord."

"Yes."

"I Eena, daughter of Clag."

As the two stared at each other curiously, some of the hostility seemed to leave him. He looked down at the meat and then shrugged. "Hungry," he said and picked it up. Using his strong white teeth, he chewed it. "Good," he said.

"That beast Lom killed. He good hunter."

The tall young warrior gazed at her admiringly. "Lom your mate?" he asked, tearing off another mouthful of meat.

Eena hesitated. "No. Someday. Not yet."

Ral's eyes flickered over the girl's dark hair, golden skin, trim form. "You skinny." Perhaps he wanted to make no kind remarks to enemies.

Eena's eyes flashed. She glowered at him and said, "You have big fat mate."

Ral laughed at that. "No. No mate. Not yet."

After a moment she asked, "You thirsty?"

"Yes."

Eena looked over at Raddy. "Go get water."

Raddy appeared insulted that a woman—even the chief's daughter—would tell him what to do. "No," he grunted.

"Then let him go to river and drink."

"No! He get away." He looked sullenly at the girl, then turned his eyes on his enemy. "He die yet. We give him to Greska."

Eena said, "*I* get water."

She soon came back bearing a cup made from a gourd, filled with clear water.

Ral drank thirstily. Then he handed back the gourd, saying, "Good."

Eena knew she should leave, but she sat down on a nearby stone anyway. "Tell me what it like where you are."

Ral was obviously surprised to be asked, but he began to tell a little of what his life was like. It was simple like her own, and Eena was astonished that there was so little difference between them. She had thought from the stories she had heard of this tribe that they were all little better than dinosaurs. And yet this young man seemed to be . . . well . . . rather nice!

They were interrupted when Lom strode up, war club in hand. He frowned at Ral and then faced Eena. "What he say?"

"He tell about his people." Eena shrugged. "They same as us."

"They *enemy*." He shook his ax at Ral, his lips drawn back from his teeth. "We enemy. We fight."

Ral said nothing, but he showed no sign of fear.

Lom was about to speak again when apparently something in the forest caught his attention. He had the alertness of a great cat, and one look seemed to tell him that the worst had happened. He let out a tremendous yell. *"Enemy! Enemy!"*

Eena jumped to her feet and saw, breaking out of the woods, a group of strange warriors armed with clubs and axes. Instantly she understood. It was Chief Mord come to save his son!

Lom's yell alerted Clag's tribe, and warriors poured down from the cave.

The Sleepers were at the river when they heard shouting.

Josh lifted his head. "What's that?"

"Sounds like trouble," Reb answered. "Come on!" He started up the path at a dead run, and the others followed.

As they approached the base of the cliff, they heard yells and grunts and screams.

"I think the war's started," Dave said, "and it didn't take arrows to do it either!"

They rounded a huge rock, and he saw a pitched battle going on.

"Look! Some of Chief Clag's men are down," Jake yelled. "We've got to help 'em."

But the youngsters' help was not needed. The attacking warriors were soon overwhelmed by Clag's fierce little band and were forced to retreat.

Lom, however, was being half carried by three of his friends. He'd taken a blow to the head and was dazed. Blood streamed down his face. "Eena!" he gasped. "Eena."

Dave caught a glimpse of the invaders disappearing into the forest, and he understood. "They've got Eena!" he yelled. He started to run, but a rope settled over his arms, and he was yanked to a stop. He whirled to see Reb. "Let me go, you crazy cowboy! We've got to save her!"

Reb held him tight. "We've got to do that all right. But you're not going to do it alone. They'd have both of you if you go."

"That's right, Dave," Josh said, "we've got to get organized."

"Who were they, Lom?" Sarah demanded. Her eyes were wide with fear.

Lom wiped the blood from his face and tried to stand. He staggered a little. "Mord—his men. They take Eena. They try get Ral."

Dave looked quickly. Ral was still tied to the tree trunk.

He had seen his father's men burst into the open, Ral said, and thought he would be rescued. But Raddy had knocked him to the ground with the flat of his ax. By the time he recovered, the raid was over and his tribesmen driven off.

Clag had been out on a hunt. When he returned an hour later and heard of the raid, his face clouded over. "They take Eena?" He walked over to Ral and shook his ax in his prisoner's face. "We kill you!"

"Don't do that!" Dave called out.

"Yes, we kill," Clag said.

But Dave began to talk rapidly. "Look, Chief, they've

got your daughter, but you've got his son. All we've got to do is go tell them we want to swap."

"Swap? What is swap?"

"It means we'll give them him—" he pointed to Ral "—and they'll give us Eena. That way you'll both get something."

Such an idea obviously had never occurred to Clag. His tribe was so fiercely independent they had nothing to do with Mord's band and were fearful of *any* strangers. The thought of even speaking to them was foreign to him.

But Dave continued to talk, and finally Beno came over. He appeared to be the one man that Clag would listen to. He was no hunter, but he was smart.

"Yes, Chief Clag. Dave right. He want son back—you want Eena back. We go to them."

Clag stared. "If we go, they kill us."

That was when Lom stepped forth. "Let *him* go," he said angrily, pointing at Dave. "Let *him* talk to Mord."

"They'd kill you, Dave," Sarah said quickly.

But Dave knew that he had no choice. He stared toward the forest where Mord's band had disappeared and then back at Clag. "All right," he said, "I'll go, Chief, but I want your word. If Mord gives us Eena, you'll give them Ral."

When Beno explained to the chief what Dave meant, Clag nodded slowly. "Yes, we give him for Eena."

"Good," Dave said. And now he tried to conceal that he was frightened. "Josh, you'll be in charge while I'm gone." He hesitated. "If I—if I don't get back, you'll know I gave it my best shot."

The Sleepers watched Dave walk swiftly away toward the wall of trees. When he disappeared, Josh said, "Well, it looks like Dave's the leader after all. I don't know if I'd have the nerve to do that."

12

The Swap

I don't think it's going to work," Josh said nervously. He had been pacing back and forth almost the entire two hours since Dave had left. More and more he had become convinced that Dave had made a mistake.

"What's the matter, Josh?" Sarah asked. "Don't you think Dave was right to go?"

"I'm not sure. We just don't know those people over there. The first man he meets might bash his brains out before he gets a chance to say a word."

Sarah bit her lip. "I've been thinking the same thing," she confessed. "But what can we do about it?"

"I haven't been able to think of anything." He looked around at the rest of the Sleepers. "Any of you have any ideas?"

"Wouldn't do any good for all of us to get together and go," Jake said logically. "All of us wouldn't be able to stand up against them any more than Dave would."

Reb shook his head doubtfully. "It's gonna be hard for him. You know what a time we had getting to be friends with Clag's people—and Mord doesn't know anything about us. I think Josh is right. They'll probably knock him in the head as soon as he appears."

A silence fell on the group.

Finally Abigail said slowly, "I think I have an idea."

They all looked at her in surprise. Abigail Roberts managed to look neat and well-groomed even living with a savage tribe. Her long blonde hair and blue eyes made her look like a beauty contestant. But Abigail, as beautiful as she was, did not often come up with great ideas.

"What is it, Abbie?" Josh asked. "Anything's better than what we've got."

She seemed to be thinking hard. "I think we ought to send Ral after Dave."

"What?" Josh exclaimed. "That's crazy!"

"Of course it is!" Jake declared indignantly. "He's the only card we've got to play. If Mord had him back, he wouldn't have to give Eena back to us."

"I don't think we're going to get her anyway," Abbie said. She shifted her shoulders nervously. "I've had a funny feeling about this—and I think the rest of you have too. I'm not the greatest planner in the world, but it seems to me, if there's any hope at all, then it'll have to come from *him*." She gestured toward Ral, who was sitting apart, his head pillowed on his arms. "If he's the chief's son, he could get her freed, I bet."

An argument ensued, but Sarah at last came over to Abbie's point of view. "I think she's right. In the first place, how's Dave ever going to find the village or cave where they live? He's probably lost right now."

Josh blinked. "I never thought of that!" he admitted.

"That's right," Reb said. "He could wander around in circles."

"And maybe get gobbled up by one of them dinosaurs," Wash added. He looked at Abbie with respect. "I think you're right, Abbie, but how do we get Ral to do it?"

"Let me talk to him," she said. She seemed a little embarrassed. "I know none of you think I have any sense, but somehow I think this is my job. It just came to me so clearly."

Josh made up his mind. "All right, you go talk to Ral. It's a long shot, but maybe it'll work."

Ral looked up as Abbie approached.

"Ral," she said, "we want you to help us."

He looked at her suspiciously. "I help *you?*"

"Yes, we want to get Eena back. You saw that Dave went after your father's warriors. He's going to offer to give you back if they'll let her go."

But Ral shook his head. "No, my father not do that. He kill your man."

"That's what we're afraid of." Abbie nodded anxiously. "But if you went and talked to your father, he'd let her go. Wouldn't he?"

"Clag no let me go."

"But if you *could* go, would you try?"

Ral seemed unable to believe what he was hearing. He shrugged, repeating, "They no let me go."

Abbie looked around. For once Raddy, the guard, was gone, and they were alone. But she would have to work fast. She pulled a small knife from her pocket. "I can cut you loose. If I do, will you tell your father to let Dave and Eena come back?"

Ral considered for only a moment, then agreed. "I try." But he looked doubtful. "My father—he hard man."

That was enough for Abbie. She began to saw at the heavy vine that bound Ral's ankle.

The sharp blade cut through it easily, and Ral was amazed. "What that?"

"It's called a knife. Here—you take it. You'll have to find Dave. He's probably lost. He doesn't know how to get to your father's village. Find him, take him there, and when he talks to your father, you help him. Make your father understand that we let *you* go."

Ral looked thoughtful, then leaped up and dashed away. He ran like a deer and disappeared into the undergrowth.

Abbie hurried back to her friends and said nervously, "He said he'd try."

"I hope he means it," Josh said. "It's going to be hard on us if he doesn't." He looked over at the cut vine rope. "Now we can start trying to explain how he got loose. Maybe we better get out of here and just let Clag's people worry about it."

"That's a good idea," Reb said. "I'm glad I thought of it!"

Dave tried to follow the signs of the band that had kidnapped Eena, but he was no tracker and soon found himself wandering aimlessly through a heavily wooded area. A branch scratched one eye, and he soon grew exhausted.

What was worse, night was coming on. Jittery, he looked around, thinking of the ferocious beasts that roamed this land, and he knew that he was helpless.

I can't even go back, he thought. *I don't know the way.* He blundered on for another half hour and then threw himself down with his back to the base of a tree, panting. He tried to think, but his mind refused to operate. Then he began to hear strange noises, some high in the treetops, others rustling in the brush. He looked behind him and thought he could see movement.

"Get hold of yourself, Dave," he said aloud. "You're going to get out of this all right. Goél didn't send you here to fail."

Suddenly a form appeared before him, and he jumped up uttering a cry of alarm. At first he thought it was a wild ape, but then—

"Ral!"

Ral apparently had trailed him easily. He probably could read the signs of a track as well as the Sleepers could read the pages of a book. He motioned to Dave and said, "Come."

"Come where?" Dave asked in bewilderment.

"To my people."

Dave was puzzled but was glad to have someone to guide him. He stumbled along after the surefooted warrior.

At last Ral said, "Too dark. We climb tree."

The tree Ral chose was huge, and Dave found climbing it difficult. Twice Ral had to reach down, grasp his wrist, and haul him up bodily. Finally they came to where the great tree intersected another, making a sort of platform. "Here. We rest till light."

Dave threw himself down on the branches, not wanting to look toward the ground far below.

The forest was almost completely dark now. Ral was nearly invisible. And as he lay there, Dave began to be aware of the noises that came out of the blackness. There were snortings and gnashings of teeth, and he was very glad to be up in the tree.

"What's going on, Ral? How did you get away?"

Ral's voice came cautiously. "Little female—Abbie. She cut me loose."

"Why? Why did she do that?"

Ral's answer was long in coming. "She say you never find my people."

"Well, she was right about that. I'd probably have been eaten by a dinosaur if you hadn't found me."

"She say my people kill you." He hesitated. "My father, hard man. Small female, she say I talk him for you. Ask for Eena go home."

Dave was stunned. *I should have thought of that.* Aloud he said, "Are you going to do it, Ral?"

But Ral did not answer. Apparently he had gone to sleep.

Dave slept by only fits and starts. He was afraid of falling, and, judging by the thrashing sounds below, there was nothing pleasant down there for him.

At first light Ral shook him awake.

The boys scrambled down the tree and soon were again threading their way through the jungle. Once they passed by a brontosaurus, bigger than a building. Ral paid no attention to him. "He eat trees," he said.

To Dave the trek seemed to take forever. They navigated several trails before finally coming to a series of stone ridges lifting out of the jungle.

Ral pointed. "My people."

Dave swallowed hard and was very glad that Ral was with him. He followed closely, and soon the pair stepped into a clearing and were surrounded by the tribe of Chief Mord.

Mord himself came forward, towering over his men. He greeted his son, who was almost as tall. "Good! You back!"

"Yes," Ral said. He motioned to Dave. "He talk."

Mord stared at Dave suspiciously and stood waiting for him to speak.

"Where is Eena?" Dave asked first.

"Here I am! Here!"

Then Dave saw her. She was sitting with two women, apparently her guards. "Are you all right, Eena?" he called.

"Yes. All right." Otherwise she remained silent, but there was gladness in her expression.

Dave turned to Mord. "Chief Mord, we come in peace."

Mord scratched his head. "Peace? What peace?"

"It means no fight," Dave answered. "No war. No kill."

A murmur went around the tribesmen, and Mord grinned suddenly. "We kill enemy. You enemy."

"No!" Ral spoke up quickly. "He not Clag's people. See, he different."

Mord seemed to understand that Dave came from a different race, but he was still suspicious. However, he listened as Dave haltingly explained that he had come to exchange Ral for Eena.

"So, you see, you have your son back, and now we ask you to give Clag's daughter back."

But Mord was shrewd. "No! I have son. We have new woman. We keep."

"But that's not fair!" Dave cried.

Mord stared. "What fair?"

"It means . . . well . . . doing what's right."

"What right?"

Dave saw that the conversation was going nowhere. He turned helplessly to the young man beside him. "Ral, you tell him."

Ral faced his father. "They let *me* go. We let *her* go."

Mord gazed at his son, seemingly trying to understand, but all this was so foreign to him that he could not. Finally, after extended talk that went around in a circle, Ral sighed and turned back to Dave. "It take—time. We wait. We see."

Dave saw that argument was useless. "All right, that's fine. Am I a prisoner?"

"What that?" Ral asked.

"I can't go back?"

"No. You stay."

Ral then went over to Eena and freed her but said to her also, "You stay."

Finally he looked at his father. "We talk."

Later that night as the tribespeople sat around the fire, Dave drifted over and seated himself close to Eena. "Your father's worried about you."

"Why your people let Ral go? He enemy of my father."

"You know Abbie? Ral says she cut him loose."

"Why?"

"They want to trade Ral for you."

Eena shook her head. "Now they have both. They no let me go."

"Maybe they will," Dave said encouragingly. "Mord's got his son back, and Ral is going to ask him to let you go."

Hope flared in the girl's eyes, and she said, "Good."

The two sat near the fire for a long time, and more than once Ral came by. He would sit with them silently, and Dave would explain what he and the Sleepers were trying to do.

He explained about Goél and how Goél called for kindness to others. "There's a better way than fighting, Ral," he said. "Goél says the best way is to treat other people just as we want them to treat us." He concluded by saying, "Your people and Eena's people—killing is not the way to go. There are even things they could do together that they can't do alone."

"What?" demanded Ral.

For the moment Dave was blank. "Well, I don't know right now, but some things. The more people you both have, the better."

Ral leaned back and stared at them. "You tell me how. I tell my father. But he hard man."

13

It's Hard to Be Friends

Somehow Dave had thought he would be welcomed by Chief Mord. After all, he had brought Ral home. It was the way he would have expected civilized people to behave. But he had miscalculated badly.

The chieftain was a fierce man, accustomed to a dog-eat-dog struggle for life. Necessity had made him suspicious, and though Ral begged him to free both Eena and Dave, he refused.

"I'm afraid it's hopeless," Dave said to her one night after nearly everyone else had gone to sleep.

The two of them were sitting as usual near the small fire. The hunters had bad luck that day, and they were hungry—as was the rest of the tribe. Dave's stomach growled, and he slapped it. "Shut up!" he said crossly. "What do you expect me to do?"

Eena giggled, and Dave was surprised. *Why, she's just like any other teenage girl,* he thought with a flash of amusement. *No, not quite. She's really different from Sarah or Abigail.*

The fire burned low, and Dave added a few sticks. The flame leaped up, casting fantastic shadows on the cave wall. All around them, the tribespeople were lying wrapped in furs. The sound of snoring rent the air, and from time to time a nightmare made someone cry out sharply.

Dave looked across the fire toward Eena who was staring into it. "We've got to get away," he said. "We've been here a week, and, if anything, Mord's more deter-mined to keep us than ever."

Eena looked up. "They watch," she whispered. "All the time, they watch." She nodded toward the guard standing at the mouth of the cave.

Dave looked at the tall warrior. "I've been watching him every night. He stays awake for a few hours, but then he always goes to sleep. Maybe he'll go to sleep tonight too."

Eena glanced around fearfully at the huge man, who was known to clutch his battle-ax even in his sleep. "He kill us if we try run away."

"He'll have to catch us first," Dave said grimly. "Now, you get some sleep, and I'll watch. I'll wake you in a couple of hours. Then we'll wait for that guard to fall asleep."

The night wore on, and the fire sank down until it was only a tiny blaze that Dave kept feeding with small sticks. He grew sleepy, but he knew that tonight might be their last chance. Hours passed, and he could hardly keep his eyes open.

Then Eena awakened and looked toward the guard, then toward Dave. "You sleep," she whispered. "I watch."

"All right," Dave grunted. He threw himself down and fell asleep at once. It seemed, however, that he had barely closed his eyes when he felt Eena's touch on his arm.

"Dave, he asleep!"

The guard was seated and nodding with his hands on his knees. He rested his forehead against them.

Dave put a finger to his lips and got to his feet. He thought, *I sure do hope he doesn't wake up!* He was wear-ing a pair of soft leather shoes. He could walk quietly. Eena had nothing at all on her feet. He saw that everyone else was still sleeping. He motioned to Eena with his head and started tiptoeing toward the cave entrance.

The closer he got, the more unlikely it seemed that they could walk right by the guard without awakening him. He slowed until he was barely moving, putting each foot down softly. When they were only a few feet away, the man coughed suddenly and stirred, rubbing his eyes.

Dave froze. He could hear the soft crackling of the blaze and the guard clearing his throat. *If he looks up,* Dave thought, *we're goners!*

But the warrior shoved his back against the wall, put his head down again, and soon began to snore.

Dave tiptoed past him, Eena close behind. Then they were outside, and Dave looked up. Fortunately there was a bright, full moon and a sky full of glittering stars. The whole landscape was bathed in soft silver light. Again he motioned, and the two made their way silently down the path to the trees.

Dave released a sigh of relief. "Come on, Eena. As soon as they find out we're gone, they'll be after us."

Eena nodded. "You know way?"

"Not too well. I know we keep going due east until we hit the river. Then we follow it north. When we get to the bluffs, we turn, and then we'll be there. Now let's go."

Dave never forgot their flight. He went at a steady trot, and Eena was right behind him. An hour later he was breathing heavily and turned to see that she was not breathing hard at all.

He tried to conceal his weariness, but she said, "You tired. We rest."

"We can't," he argued.

But she insisted. They sat down on a log, and he was glad for the relief.

"You think they catch?" she asked anxiously.

"No, I don't think so. I believe you'll be home safe with your tribe and your father soon."

Eena sat silently then. The soft silver moonlight washed over her attractive face. After a while she said, "They no bad people."

Dave looked at her with surprise. "They'll kill us if they catch us!"

"They afraid," she said. "*We* afraid. But they no bad people."

Dave thought about that insight, but there was little time for thinking. After fifteen minutes he arose and said, "We've got to keep going, Eena."

They kept up the pace all night, and when morning broke they came to the river.

"We're all right now, I think." Dave sighed again with relief. "Let's try to get to the cave before the sun gets high. We might run into a t-rex. I'd hate to get eaten by one of those things just when we got away."

They followed the river, crossed over at a ford, and when the sun was a quarter of the way up in the sky they arrived at the base of The People's caves.

The first to see them was Wash. He was watching Reb plow with the ox, Stonewall, and he let out a shrill yelp. "Look! There they come! It's Dave and Eena!"

His yell must have roused the camp. As the pair walked in, it seemed they were surrounded by everyone in the tribe. Dave's face flushed with pleasure as his friends beat him on the shoulders, praising him for bringing Eena home.

But it was Chief Clag who was most pleased. Beaming, he took his daughter by the arm and shook her fondly. "You back!"

"Yes. Dave—he bring back."

"Good. Dave, good." Clag gave the witch doctor a harsh look, and the man slunk away without a single word about Greska. "We celebrate. We have feast." He sud-

120

denly clapped a hand on Dave's back that nearly collapsed him.

Dave coughed and then said, "Well, I'm glad I was able to do something, Chief."

Later they did have a time of feasting, for the hunting that day had been good. Dave was asked to tell the story of how he overcame all the tribesmen of Mord.

"How many you kill?" Clag demanded.

"Well . . as a matter of fact, none," Dave said.

Disappointment washed across the Chief's face. "How many you kill?" he repeated.

"None, Chief. We ran away when the guard went to sleep."

Lom laughed aloud. "A woman do that much," he said. But he closed his mouth when Clag gave him a stern word.

After the feast was over, the Seven Sleepers gathered together, and Josh said, "Now, tell it like it really was, Dave. How'd you do it?"

Dave shrugged. "Nothing heroic about it. We tried to talk Chief Mord into letting us go, but he was suspicious like all these savages are. He would have kept us there forever. So when the guard went to sleep, we just ran away."

"I got an idea we're gonna be visited," Reb said. "Mord won't like it, your getting away with Eena like that. Probably figured she was his property."

A murmur of assent went around.

Sarah said, "We've *got* to teach these people how to trust each other—to treat each other the way they want to be treated."

Dave said abruptly, "Well, that's what I thought, but it's impossible, Sarah. They're just too backward. The best we can do is help them learn how to plow a little.

Maybe plant some grain." He shrugged. "Maybe in a few years they'll learn how to stop killing each other."

"That's why Goél sent us," Josh said. "To teach these people how to trust him and one another and do what's right."

Wash looked at him strangely. "Yeah, but these people are different. They don't trust very easy. Back in Oldworld, I remember growing up—white people and black people didn't always get along." He looked over at Reb and grinned, his white teeth flashing. "Now, me and Reb, we get along fine, but it was hard to learn, wasn't it, Reb?"

"Sure was." Reb nodded. "These people are more suspicious than I ever thought anybody could be. They just don't like anybody that's not part of them. And they never even think about treating other folks the way they'd like to be treated. You may be right, Dave."

Dave arose the next morning with a new determination. He went to see Beno.

"The people need something to protect themselves from the wild animals. You start making arrowheads. I'll get everybody else to make bows. If we get enough arrows, we could put down a pretty good-sized dinosaur— maybe even a young T-rex."

"The big killer with jaws? That be something. Yes, I work."

For the next two weeks the Sleepers were kept busy, and so were any of the tribesmen that had a gift for shaping bows or whittling arrows. Soon they had a plentiful supply, and Dave trained many of the warriors to do an adequate job of shooting. All day long one could hear their cries as they practiced and either hit or missed.

One day Eena stopped by and watched Beno make arrowheads. He appeared surprised. Usually she watched the warriors practice shooting. She sat down across from him and watched as he continued to pound off splinters of flint.

"I no see how you do that, Beno." She herself had tried many times to make an arrowhead, but she had never succeeded. She smiled. "Without you, they no have arrows."

Beno flushed.

She knew he was not accustomed to being praised. Certainly not by her. She also knew he had admired her from afar. And now he was looking again at her hair, her eyes, her long, straight limbs.

He mumbled, "I no hunt."

Eena had been brought up to revere hunters above all, but somehow she had gained a little wisdom in these past few weeks. She put a hand on Beno's shoulder and smiled. "You very good man, Beno. Very smart. You make anything." She thought a moment and said, "You most important man in tribe—except my father."

Beno stared at her unbelievingly. He ducked his head, so embarrassed was he.

Eena laughed at him. "You make me more necklace sometime?" She touched the bone necklace around her neck that Beno had carved painstakingly. It was the only jewelry in the tribe, and she was very proud of it.

Beno smiled. "I make more. It look good on you."

She stared at him. He was a nice-looking young man, she thought. Not as strong, of course, as the other young men, but he had attractive brown hair and brown eyes and —except that one leg was a little smaller than the other— was rather handsome, she suddenly decided.

"You come," she said. "I show you field. Maybe you make better way to grind grain so we make bread."

All day the Seven Sleepers had worked hard making

123

arrow shafts and awkwardly scraping bows with the stones Beno had formed.

That night Dave said, "I can't see that we're doing much good in this place. I don't know what else Goél could expect of us."

The others were tired also and almost as discouraged as he was.

Sarah said, "Maybe it's time to go back. Maybe we've done what we came to do."

Dave looked up. "I think that's right. We'd better think about leaving pretty soon."

For the next four days all the Sleepers talked about leaving. Things seemed to be at a standstill. Then one morning, after they had washed in the creek and were sitting around talking, Dave said, "We'll give it another week. Then we'll go back."

Josh bit his lip. "I hate to get beaten like this. Seems like we just haven't helped these people much."

"Maybe we've helped them more than you think," Jake said. "We taught them how to plow, and Reb taught them how to domesticate animals. They can have their own livestock now. And they can bake bread."

"I know," Josh said doubtfully, "but—"

He never finished his sentence for there was a loud cry and a figure emerged from the woods.

"That looks like Ral!" Dave exclaimed. He waited until the man got nearer. "It *is* Ral! Let's see what's up!"

They all ran to meet the young man, who was breathing hard.

"What is it, Ral? What's wrong?" Dave demanded.

"I come for you." He could barely speak, and he sucked in great lungfuls of air. "Many-toothed lizards come."

That was his word, Dave knew, for dinosaur, and at once a chill went over him.

"What about your people?"

"They in trees, in caves with stones, but lizards come! Many!" He held up his fingers twice to indicate about twenty.

"What do you want us to do?" Dave asked.

"You come! You help my people!"

By this time, Chief Clag arrived with his warriors and the medicine man. The women also gathered around.

"What *he* do here?" Clag demanded.

Dave explained the situation and ended by saying. "He wants us to help him—help his people."

Clag looked at him as if he had lost his mind, and Dave saw at once that this was not going to be easy.

Ral walked straight up to the chief. He kneeled down in front of him and said, "You make me slave. I do anything. Only help my people."

A murmur went over the crowd, and a strange look came into the chief's eyes. But he grasped his battle-ax and shook his head. "We no help!"

Then Eena came. She took her father's arm—a rare gesture for her—and said, "Someday maybe *we* need help. We help them now. They help *us* later."

Such an idea probably had never occurred to her father. For the next hour there was another fierce debate over what to do. Once again, the tribe was divided.

At length Clag said, "This many lizards? They kill us all."

"No," Dave said. "No, not if we use the arrows."

"How big are these lizards?" Josh asked. He was afraid that Ral would say they were T-rexes.

But Ral held his hand at about a level of his own head. "This big," he said. "Big teeth. Big claws on feet."

"They're bad ones," Reb said. "We've seen what they can do. I believe enough of them could take down a big dinosaur."

125

The debate ended when a determined Clag said, "We no go." He looked around fiercely. "No one go. We take care our people. They not our people."

14
What Would Goél Do?

The Sleepers drew to one side, as was their custom when dealing with any matter. They found a place beside the river to meet. Josh had insisted on bringing Ral along.

As soon as they got there, Josh said, "I know you're the leader, Dave, but I think we need to talk about this."

A stubborn look came into Dave's face. "There's nothing to talk about. I've decided Clag is right. It would be pretty close to suicide to try to help Ral's people."

"What about those bows and arrows you've been working on?" Reb demanded. "You've been talking about how great they are. I believe they'd stop one of those lizards."

"And I've been thinking about that. In the hands of a good bowman, they would. But these men haven't used them except for target practice. When they look down the throat of a dinosaur, I think most of them would turn and run."

"They've got more nerve than that," Jake said abruptly. "I believe we ought to try to get the chief and all the warriors to go help."

The argument went on for some time, and finally Dave grew impatient. "No, it's too late to try to help. I'm sorry for your father and your people, Ral, but we wouldn't do any good if we did go."

Ral had been listening carefully. Now he looked into Dave's face and, without a word, walked away.

"Where are you going, Ral?" Josh called out.

"Back. Die with my people."

Wash ran quickly to his side. "Wait. Let us talk a little more. Don't go yet."

Dave said, "You can talk all you want to, but we're not going back to Mord's country, and that's final!" He walked off, aware that he was behaving badly.

He didn't want to talk to anyone, so he took the river path and lost himself in the shade of the huge trees that reached high overhead. The sun was growing hot, but it was cool under here. He walked along, once noticing a crocodile or something like a crocodile that must have been at least fifty feet long. He shivered to think what those mighty jaws would do and then continued walking.

He came to a tree that hung over the river, and he leaned against it. The water was so clear he could see the silver fish. He watched them for a while, troubled and unhappy. He picked up a stone, tossed it in, and watched the fish scurry away, disappearing with a twinkling of their silver scales.

He picked up another rock, held it, looked at it, then said aloud, "I don't want anything bad to happen to Ral's people." His speech shattered the silence of the place. "Maybe I'm just afraid. I wonder if that's it."

He thought of the dinosaurs with their rows of razor-keen teeth and those huge, sharp claws on the back of each foot that could disembowel a horse. He shuddered to think what it would be like to fall into their jaws.

Troubled that he might be a coward, Dave began to walk once again along the river path. At last he sat down on a rock, feeling even more despondent. He was about ready to get up and return when a voice said, "The hour is late, David."

Dave jumped up and whirled—and there was Goél, standing in the shadows!

"Goél!" he gasped. "Is it really you?"

Goél did not move. Where they stood was murky twilight, and his face was indistinct.

Dave asked, rather foolishly, "How did you get here? Have you come to take us back?"

There was a silence, and then Goél said gently, "Is it time to go back, David?"

Instantly Dave felt shame running through him. He dropped his head and chewed his lip. He didn't know what to say, and he let the silence run on. Finally he whispered, "You'd better get someone else to lead the group, Goél. I'm no good at it."

Goél didn't answer for a moment. When he did, his voice was almost a whisper. "You are the servant of Goél, David. You have a good name, and you have a good heart. A bit stubborn at times, and you tend to be proud."

"I know," Dave said shamefacedly. "I'm sorry, Goél. And I'll apologize to the others."

"That's my good lad," Goél said more warmly. "I must leave you now." He stepped back in the shadows, and now his voice did come as a mere whisper. "Do what is right. Do what you would want someone else to do for you."

Dave blinked. "Goél!" He followed his visitor into the dense thicket, but he found no trace of him.

"Was I dreaming?" Then his jaw tightened. "Even if I *was* dreaming, I know what to do. Do what is right, rather than run away like I've been doing!"

He raced back up the path. He stumbled into a small covey of pterodactyls, who rose up, their leather wings flapping, their long beaks opening and closing as they uttered harsh cries. Dave paid them no heed.

He found the other Sleepers and Ral in the place where he had left them. When he came up to them, he stopped and caught his breath. Then he said, "I've been wrong. Maybe we'll all get killed—I don't know—but I know what Goél wants us to do. We've got a chance here to show these people what helping others is. That's what they don't understand." He turned to Ral. "Ral, I'm sorry that I let you down. But now I'm going to do all I can to help your father and all your people. We're going to give your people the kind of help we'd like to have ourselves if *we* were in trouble."

Reb jerked off his hat, threw it high in the air, and let out a loud Rebel yell. *"Whooeee!* Now we're gonna see something! Let's get this show on the road!"

Dave held up a hand. "First, we've got to convince the chief to send his men. Let's go do it."

"What if they won't go?" Abigail said fearfully.

Dave looked at her and said, "Well, then, we'll just have to go by ourselves. The Seven Sleepers have come to the kingdom, I think, for such a time as this."

15

Attack on the Dinosaurs

Dave had little hope that Clag would send his warriors to help his deadly enemies. He knew well the bitterness between the two tribes. But he believed that Goél had given him a commission, and he now did not hesitate for one moment.

He led his friends, accompanied by Ral, to where the chief was meeting with his most trusted warriors.

Dave approached him and said, "Chief Clag, we have come to help your people." He paused, then went on. "We have done little so far. But if we could do just one thing more, it would be the best thing that ever happened to the people of Clag."

"What that?" Clag demanded.

Dave looked him straight in the eye. "You are not alone here. There are others in this world. Everywhere there are people, and a Dark Power is sweeping over the land. There is evil, and evil always destroys everything it touches."

"What this evil? It your god?"

"No! Our Goél is good! Man's heart—that is where evil lies."

"I not hate my people," Clag said. "I chief. I protect them." He looked into the distance where all knew Mord's band lay. "We fight Mord. They kill us, we kill them. Only strong stay alive."

"That's what you've always done. But there's a better way, the way Goél has instructed us to tell you."

For a long time, Dave stood explaining, as the sun beat down on his head. The villagers came out from the cave and up from the river where they had been fishing. Soon the whole village surrounded him.

He spoke about the need for trust and love. He talked about treating others the way Clag would want to be treated. He looked at the chief. "Is this not good, Clag?"

Clag's face turned toward his people, and Dave saw many heads nod in agreement.

"Yes," the chief said at last. "Mord's people need friend to help."

"That's exactly right." Dave waved a hand toward the village and beyond. "Mord needs help. His people are like yours. Women will cry because their men are dead. Some of the women will die. They care for their women and their children just as you do. They love even as you love your own."

While he waited, Dave could hear Josh and Sarah murmuring behind him.

"I never knew Dave could talk like that," Josh said in admiration. "Goél did right to choose him as leader."

"Do you think Clag will listen?" Sarah asked doubtfully.

"I think so. Look! Here comes Eena—she's going to ask him to go. He thinks the world of that girl, though he doesn't show it much."

"Please," Eena begged her father. "We help!"

No one could ever explain afterward how it happened, but somehow a change came over the chief. Dave could almost see it happening. His face, which had been hard, grew soft as he looked at his daughter. And whether it was her "Please" or the idea that fascinated him, no one could ever say. But he suddenly lifted his ax and said, "We go help." Then he turned to Ral. "Lead us. We help your people."

132

At once a shrill yell arose, and then all the warriors began screaming. It was very confusing for a while, but finally Dave got their attention.

"Wait! Wait! We've got to use the bows and arrows. I don't know if they'll stop a dinosaur or not, but we'll find out."

Reb said, "I got an idea. What do you think of this?" And he outlined a strategy he had dreamed up. There was a fighting quality in Reb. Back at Camelot he had put some of the strongest men flat on their backs, and now his light blue eyes blazed as he explained his plan.

"I think it'll work," Wash said. "Let's try it."

A cry went up again, and Dave saw that everyone was with him. "OK, everybody get armed! Let's go!"

The band had traveled hard and now was coming close to the village of Mord.

Ral held up a hand and said, "Animals, they over there." He pointed to a small rise and shook his head. "They many." He held up both hands again, indicating twenty.

Reb said, "OK, let's try this little plan of mine." He was riding the young ox, Stonewall. He carried with him a mass of vine ropes, and now he pulled at the harness he had arranged over Stonewall's legs and body.

"The secret is," he said, "we've got to get those rascals one at a time. Let's do it like I said."

Dave said, "I'll go first. They're right over there, you say, Ral?"

"Yes."

"All right, spread out." Dave grinned at Reb. "I hope this works."

"Got to work," Reb said confidently. His eyes were searching the trees. Then he pointed to a limb about ten feet off the ground. "That one right there will do. You bring one of them critters through here, and we'll get him."

Dave ran down the path, and as soon as he came to an opening his heart almost stopped. Dinosaurs were roaming about, uttering sharp, fierce cries. Some were reaching into the trees where Mord and his people were clinging to branches. Some were at a cave mouth, trying to get at those who seemed to be barricaded inside.

Dave approached slowly, his heart in his throat. They were ferocious-looking reptiles—not large, but they moved very fast. "I hope I can outrun them," he muttered.

He pulled out a handkerchief and waved it.

Instantly the closest dinosaur turned toward him, letting out a piercing cry.

Dave waved the handkerchief again, and the dinosaur charged. He whirled and dashed back up the path. "Here he comes, Reb! Don't miss!"

He glimpsed Reb off to one side beneath the tree he'd chosen. A lariat loop was hanging over a branch. Four of Mord's strongest warriors held the other end.

"Ready," Reb shouted. "When I holler, you pull."

Dave flashed by, the dinosaur right on his tail. He had not known a reptile could move so rapidly.

"Run, Dave, run!" Josh yelled.

Then, as the creature thundered past, Reb tossed the noose over its head and short, stubby front legs. "Pull! *Pull!*" he yelled.

The four warriors hauled on the vine rope with all their might. The noose closed around the dinosaur's middle.

The men sagged under the strain, but now Lom too called, "Pull! Pull!" and they threw their strength into it. The dinosaur was suddenly yanked up into the air. He squalled and clawed, but his stumpy legs could not reach the lariat.

"All right, you archers!" Dave yelled. "Let him have it!"

Instantly a dozen of Clag's best archers stepped out of the woods and drew their bows.

Twang! Twang! Twang!

A few arrows missed, but the beast was punctured by many of them. He struggled briefly, then went limp.

"You've got him!" Reb screamed. "Let that critter down! Get them arrows out!"

"We've got this thing whipped," Josh said exultantly. "Let me go get another one."

Before Dave could answer, Josh was sprinting down the path to perform the same operation. Moments later he reappeared, a dinosaur on his heels. He shouted, "Don't miss, Reb!"

Soon that reptile too was lassoed, strung up, and pierced with arrows. Cries of joy went up from all the tribesmen.

Clag stared as if he couldn't believe what he was seeing. He came over to Dave and said, "Good! Good! Now me."

One by one the warriors and the Sleepers took turns —even Wash, small as he was—luring the dinosaurs. The trick was to get only one of them to come at a time.

When just three were left, Beno, who had begged to come along, said, "Now me."

All the warriors looked at each other. Beno had never been on a hunt. He was small, almost frail, but there was a determined light in his eye.

Clag nodded. "You go, Beno."

And Beno hobbled down the trail.

When he disappeared, Dave said worriedly, "He can't run fast enough. We'll probably have to help him. Everybody grab a bow! Get your arrows notched!"

His advice was well taken for when Beno came hobbling back, two lizards were close behind him.

"No time for lassos!" Dave yelled. "Pepper those lizards!"

The air suddenly was filled with whizzing arrows. As before, some missed, but Dave had the satisfaction of seeing his own arrow go right into the open mouth of one beast. The frightening creature fell.

The second dinosaur, however, though struck several times, had almost caught up to Beno.

And then Beno fell.

"Oh, no!" Dave yelled. He had no arrows left, nor had most of the other hunters.

And then Ral did something Dave simply could not believe. He had no bow, but he had his battle-ax. Uttering a shrill cry, he leaped over the fallen Beno and charged the giant lizard. He brought his ax down with a tremendous blow that took the dinosaur in the skull. The reptile fell to the ground.

Then a cry of victory arose, and the chief himself went to the son of his old enemy and put a hand on his shoulder. "You brave warrior! You great chief one day," he said.

"Just one more left!" Dave yelled then. "Come on, we can take him!"

Clag's people had recovered enough of their arrows now, and the whole band went boiling out of the woods into the plain. The dinosaur took one look at them and attacked. But he had not taken more than five rapid steps when a dozen arrows pierced him. He let out a series of short cries and lay still.

Dave looked up into the trees where Mord's tribesmen were hanging on for dear life. Then he turned and said, "Chief Clag, I think you should ask them to come down."

136

Clag looked up and saw his enemy Mord. He looked at the arrows that his hunters had recovered.

For one awful instant, Dave thought, *He's going to kill them all!*

But then Eena came up beside her father. She smiled. And this seemed to decide Chief Clag. He said, "Come down. Lizards all dead."

Mord dropped to the ground, apparently half expecting to be killed. "You no kill us?"

Clag shook his head. "No."

"Why?"

Clag put his hand suddenly on Ral's shoulder. "You have brave son." He looked Mord in the eye. "You brave man. We no kill each other anymore."

Ral said to his father, "They come to help. Next time, maybe we help *them*."

Mord looked at his old enemy Clag, then around at his people, who were coming down from the trees, all safe. Slowly he nodded, and a small smile touched his lips. He looked at Ral. "We be good friends these people, my son."

Ral nodded eagerly. "Yes, no kill. We help each other."

Josh put a hand on Dave's arm. "Well, that's what Goél sent us to do. You've done a fine job, Dave. No one could have done better."

Dave looked down, and for one moment his lip quivered. "You'll never know," he said, "how close I came to making the biggest mistake of my life."

Josh said, "I've been there. Awful, isn't it? But you followed Goél instead. That's all that counts."

Looking around, Dave saw that the two tribes were moving closer together, looking at each other, beginning to talk. Then the Sleepers gathered around him, and he said, "I think our work's just about done here."

"Not before we have supper," Reb announced defiantly.

"Are you really going to eat them lizards?" Jake demanded.

"Why, I et a iguana once. It wasn't bad."

"You ate a *lizard?*" Wash demanded. "What'd it taste like?"

Reb thought for a moment. "I guess more like bobcat than anything else."

16

You Never Know
About a Woman

Somehow we always know when it's time to leave a
place, don't we?" Dave was speaking thoughtfully to
his six companions. "We knew when it was time to leave
Atlantis, and we knew when it was time to leave Camelot."

"I guess that's right," Josh said. He looked over to
where Clag's and Mord's tribes had come together for
their first annual feast. "I'd say, on the whole we've done
a pretty good job."

Reb nodded firmly. "I taught 'em how to rope and
how to ride. We taught 'em how to plow, how to keep
herds and goats, and how to make bread."

"Yeah! And how to make bows and arrows to protect
themselves," Wash added. "I don't think they're gonna kill
each other now."

Jake was watching the festivities. "I never thought
I'd see this, the way they hated each other. Look at them.
They all look like they're eating at a county fair."

Sarah had been noticing something else. "And have
you all noticed what's happening with Eena?"

"What's that?" Josh said in surprise.

Sarah drew her lips tight together. "I don't believe
you'd notice if a mountain fell on top of you, Joshua Adams."

Josh looked bewildered. "I don't know what you're
talking about."

"Why, it's Ral and Lom. They're both interested in her. Can't you see that?"

Abigail sniffed. "He's blind as a bat," she announced. "It's plain as the nose on your face that pretty soon they're going to fight. The winner will get her."

"Well, that'd be a pretty good scrap," Jake said. "Those are two strong guys. I don't know who I'd bet on."

"Maybe it won't happen," Dave said. "I've tried to teach Eena a little bit about courtship."

"Oh?" Sarah looked at him sharply. "I didn't know you were such an expert in such things, Dave."

"Aw, all he ever did before we come here was read them advice-to-the-lovelorn columns." Reb grinned.

It turned out that Sarah and Abbie were right. Later that afternoon, Ral and Lom stood facing one another. Obviously the two were both enamored of Eena, and suddenly they were at each other's throats, rolling in the dust. The tribespeople gathered around, encouraging their favorites.

"Somebody's going to be pretty well scratched up," Jake said. "Those guys mean business."

The fight went on until both young men were bloodied and exhausted, scarcely able to see, so swollen were their faces.

Clag and Mord both seemed to enjoy the fight, but it was Clag who finally called a halt to it. "Which you want, Eena?"

Eena stared at the two warriors, and a silence fell over the gathering.

Josh leaned over and whispered to Dave, "She'll pick Ral. See if she doesn't."

"No, she won't either," Dave whispered back. "She's always liked Lom. She'll pick him."

"How much would you bet?" Sarah asked.

"Anything you want," Josh said confidently.

"Yeah, anything you want," Dave echoed.

"If you're right," Sarah said, "—either one of you —I'll wait on you both all the way back home, cook your food, wash your clothes, take care of you like kings."

"Hey, that sounds good! I'll take that bet." Josh grinned. "We can't lose."

"We can't lose," Dave said. "I'll take it."

"But if I pick the right one, then you two wait on me, carry my things, cook for me, and do anything I say?"

"Sure, sure," both boys agreed. "Which one do you say?"

Sarah leaned over and whispered a name.

They both stared at her, and Josh laughed aloud. "I thought you had more good sense than that, Sarah." He winked at Dave. "It's gonna be pretty nice being pampered, isn't it, old buddy?"

"Sure is." Dave nodded.

They all turned to look at Eena, who had now risen. Obviously enjoying the attention she was receiving, she went to the two bloodied young men. She smiled at each of them—then walked on to where Beno stood. She took his arm, then turned to look at her father. "Beno—I be his mate."

A mutter ran around the crowd, and Sarah said sweetly, "It looks like I'm going to have an easy trip back, doesn't it?"

Josh and Dave exchanged dismayed glances, and misery crept into Josh's eyes. "We're in trouble, Dave. I can tell you that right now!"

The sun was going down as the Seven Sleepers made their way along the trail. They had said their good-byes to both tribes, and although many had urged them to return, they had merely said, "It's as Goél commands."

Now, on this second day of their journey, Sarah glanced back to see Josh trudging along under a double burden, her gear and his too. She had had a delightful time the previous day, strolling along as the two boys carried her burdens, then resting while they cooked her food and brought it to her.

Now Josh had fallen behind, and she waited until he caught up. He sat down heavily beside the trail. "How much longer you going to keep this up, Sarah?"

She sat down beside him. "Keep what up?"

He stared at her. "You know what I'm talking about. Making me do all this work—wait on you hand and foot!"

"That was the bet, wasn't it?"

Josh stared at her curiously. "How did you know that—that Eena would choose Beno?"

"She told me."

"She *told* you! And you let us think—"

Sarah began to laugh. She had been holding back her laughter all the time, and now she let it ring out.

Josh's mouth fell open. Then he got up and started down the path again.

Sarah let him get twenty feet away before she got up. "Josh, don't be angry—"

A sudden snort came from her right. She whirled to see a scaly, scary-looking dinosaur, not large, not much bigger than a small pig. But it was coming right toward her!

Sarah screamed and made a dive for a tree. The lowest branch was over her head, almost too high to reach, but she seized it with both hands. She was not strong enough to pull herself all the way up. She looked down and saw the scaly animal rising on its hind legs, coming for her feet. She braced them against the tree trunk.

"Josh!" she shrieked. "Help! He's going to eat me!"

Josh came back slowly, a grin on his face. "Yes," he said solemnly, "I believe he is."

"What is it, Josh? What is it?"

"This is a *Terribilus Animalas*. Very dangerous," he declared.

"Get him away! Get him away, Josh! Kill him!"

Josh said, "If I do, will you let me off the bet?"

"Yes, yes! Anything! I promise."

Josh walked up to the small animal—which was more the size of an overgrown armadillo than a dinosaur—and gave it a hearty kick. "Get out of here!" he said. The animal snorted and ran.

Sarah dropped to the ground. She faced Josh and said, "That wasn't a dangerous animal. That was just an old herb-eater."

"But remember what you said." He took off her pack and handed it to her.

"I think you're mean!" She put the pack on and trudged away. He came up beside her. After a while he said, "You never know what a woman will do. I sure thought Eena would take Lom or Ral."

Sarah was pouting a little, but she shook her head. "I knew she wouldn't. She's a smart girl. She could see what's coming."

"What *is* coming?" Josh asked, a perplexed look on his face.

"I think she's looking for a different kind of man, one that would be gentle and take care of her. You saw how some of the women were treated. Beno would never treat his wife like that. He's really very sweet."

They plodded on for a while, then Josh said, "Well, I hope they'll be happy."

Sarah reached out suddenly and took his hand. "Beno is sweet—like you, Josh."

"Me?" He looked down at the hand in his, and his face flushed. "You never called me *that* before."

Sarah smiled at him and squeezed his hand. "Didn't I? Well, it's true enough. Don't you have something nice to say about me?"

Josh appeared to be searching his brain. "Well, you don't sweat much—"

Sarah's face froze. She jerked her hand away and stalked off.

"Wait a minute, Sarah! Wait a minute!" He caught up with her. "You didn't let me finish. You don't sweat much, and you're the prettiest girl I ever saw!"

Sarah turned back and smiled, looking up at the tall, gangling boy. Taking his hand again, she whispered, "You know, Josh Adams, you do have your moments!"

Moody Press, a ministry of the Moody Bible Institute, is designed for education, evangelization, and edification. If we may assist you in knowing more about Christ and the Christian life, please write us without obligation: Moody Press, c/o MLM, Chicago, Illinois 60610.